HERE TODAY GONE TOMATO

MEXICAN MYSTERIES COZY MYSTERY SERIES
BOOK 2

MONA MARPLE

In January 2022, my mother sadly passed away.
I dedicate this book to her memory.
She was a lover of cozy mysteries, borrowing as many as she
could from the library.
I have wonderful memories of days spent with her, watching
Miss Marple, Poirot, Midsomer Murders and more.
Love and miss you, mum x

1
_____

I'd never seen a hotel like it. Sure, the last place had
been impressive in a business trip kind of way, but the
Kennedy Resort Grand was like something from a
child's imagination.

Seven pools. A lifesize pirate ship in the middle of one -
I'd even heard it had a tiki bar inside! Four restaurants.
Direct beach access. Fireworks every Friday.

And somehow, Uncle Cornelius had bagged us the Opal
Suite, a two bedroom palatial space with a huge balcony, hot
tub and the best view of the fireworks.

It was on that balcony that I sat, looking out at the aqua-
marine ocean as the sun glinted off the waves.

Four whole days stretched ahead of me. Days with
nothing to do and nowhere to be, which was handy as Uncle
C seemed incapable of being anywhere on time.

I took another sip of my chilled water and closed my
eyes. I enjoyed the feel of the warm sun on my bare legs, and
couldn't wait to slip into one of the pools.

"You're not sleeping, are you, lassie?" The boom of
Cornelius' voice tore me away from my peaceful thoughts

and I opened my eyes and smiled at my uncle, who was dressed in neon yellow shorts and a Hawaiian shirt.

"Wow, you're quite the sight for sore eyes! I'm not sleeping, Uncle. How could I? I'm just enjoying the sun. I can't believe this place. Did my mum really come here?" I asked.

Cornelius nodded, and his impressive moustache danced along. "I'll tell you the story. I promise. But first, my stomach advises me that it fears starvation!"

I laughed. "We only ate an hour ago!"

"That was a mere snack."

"Ok! What do you fancy?" I asked. Talking Cornelius out of eating was an impossible job. Plus, I was curious to explore the resort and see what the restaurants had to offer.

"Everything! I fancy everything! And tonight, lassie, we dine at the chef's table!"

"The chef has a table? Won't he be busy in the kitchen?" I asked, my tone earnest and my eyes wide.

Something about my question caused Cornelius to grab his barrel of a stomach and erupt into laughter. His face, or the small part of it visible in between all of his facial hair, grew red, then purplish, as the laughter contorted into a coughing fit.

"Are you okay?" I asked as I jumped up from the chair and prepared to attempt CPR. The fact that I had no idea how to perform CPR was beside the point. I'd seen it done a few times on TV and considered myself a quick learner.

Cornelius batted me away as he calmed down and his skin returned to its normal colour.

"I'll finish getting ready and then we'll go?"

"Sure!" I exclaimed, and I followed my uncle back into the mammoth suite.

～

FORTY MINUTES LATER, CORNELIUS' room looked like a bomb site. An explosion of bright shirts and garish shorts lay abandoned in piles all over the tiled floor, and the man himself gazed upon the mess, his body wrapped in a luxurious waffle towel.

"It's no good. I must have left the flamingo one on Janitzio Island. How could I be such an oaf?"

"Don't be hard on yourself. We've all done similar. And you've got plenty of lovely things to wear," I reassured him. Unlike Uncle C, I really only had had a snack earlier, and my stomach was beginning to grumble.

"I'll be a few more minutes, lassie. I need to make an impression. But you don't have to wait around for me."

"I wouldn't mind a walk. Shall I go and explore? See you at reception in a half hour?"

Cornelius guffawed. "Half an hour?! I'll only be a minute! Why, Emily, I was once awarded the prestigious title of Fastest Dresser. Back in '67. Now that was a year. In fact... oh, that can wait. You get off and explore!"

"Are you sure?" I asked.

"Yes, yes! There'll be some fine looking men in the bar! Don't take your purse, they'll be fighting over the chance to buy you a mojito."

My cheeks flushed. I'd never been bought a drink in my life and felt sure tonight would be no different. I did want to go and see what the hotel resort had to offer, though, and so I grabbed my little handbag and called out a fond farewell towards my uncle's messy lair.

As soon as I opened the door of the suite and stepped into the corridor, relaxing music soothed me. If there were speakers piping the music in, they were invisible to my naked eyes. Although, knowing the hotel, there was every chance that there were real musicians employed on every floor to play throughout the day and night.

I took a deep breath and pulled out I mobile phone. My dad wouldn't believe where I was, and I felt a sudden urge to share the experience with him. I dialled the familiar number, and listened to the line ring once, twice, all the way to the voicemail greeting.

I smiled involuntarily at dad's awkward tone as he directed me to leave a message after the beep, but then I ended the call. I wanted to speak to my father, not his inbox. I tucked the phone back in the small bag and continued to walk down the endlessly long corridor, towards the lifts.

When the door opened, a small, neat woman with a dark pixie haircut was already in there, tapping away on her own phone with an impressive concentration. She didn't seem to even notice me walk in.

As the door closed, the woman's phone rang and she answered it before it got to the second ring. I watched from the corner of my eye. I had never seen such a flawless looking person, and felt certain that I was in the presence of someone important.

Then, I rolled my eyes at myself. The Kennedy Resort Grand must be full of important people!

"Yes, it's LuAnn. Who else would be answering my phone?" the woman barked into the device.

I averted my eyes. I hated confrontation and even listening in to someone else's made me feel uncomfortable.

"No, I haven't spoken to him. He should be arriving anytime but his plans really aren't my concern anymore. Did you speak to Wayne?"

I busied myself by reaching into my bag and pulling out my own phone. It was an older model, with nothing much I could do to occupy the time other than play snake, but at least I could appear to be doing something other than listening in to a private conversation. Not that I had much of a choice in such a small space.

The lift seemed to be taking a long time.

"You need to choose the floor. Excuse me? You haven't pressed the button for the floor you want," the woman said, and it took a few moments for me to realise that I was being spoken to.

"Oh! Gosh, I'm sorry, I thought it had already been pressed," my cheeks flushed as I reached across and selected the ground floor.

"I just go up and down for fun," the woman said, but I wasn't sure whether she was joking or telling the truth, or even if she was still addressing me or had gone back to her phone call.

"He went for it? Well, that's good. We need to work on numbers. Did you see last week's number two? Some show about giraffes giving birth. Apparently they live streamed the whole thing. What's wrong with people? Who would want to watch that? What? Oh, well, that's a good point. Ha! Okay, and the table's booked when?"

I tried to concentrate on my round of snake, but my mind wandered. Whoever LuAnn was, she was a frenetic ball of energy. Maybe in her 50s, although she had that ageless look that came with a certain level of wealth and plastic surgery. Hers was a face that suggested not just the most expensive face creams and a Botox habit, but also an assistant to prepare meals and a lifetime of flying First Class, where the cabin crew provided facial misting spray and silk pyjamas.

It was so different from my own upbringing that I couldn't but feel curious about it, even as I was fairly certain that I wouldn't have wanted it for myself.

The lift reached the ground floor and the doors opened.

"Thank you," I said, and looked across at LuAnn with a smile. LuAnn smiled back, then attempted to furrow her brow, but her brow would not be furrowed. Only then did I wonder why I had thanked LuAnn; it wasn't as if she was the lift operator. I could be such a dork.

But as I watched, LuAnn appeared to take me in, to assess me in a way that made me feel as though I was naked. LuAnn seemed to look at me and see right through to my soul.

"You really have got wonderful..." LuAnn began to say, but then the lift door closed, and I wasn't sure whether the woman had been speaking to me, never mind what the end of the sentence would have been.

I shook the moment away and got my bearings. The grand reception desk was in front of me, and it was as breathtaking a sight as it had been when Uncle C and I had arrived to check in. The staff wore immaculate uniforms, the reception area featured large, plush velvet settees, and the ceiling twinkled as the light bounced off a huge crystal chandelier.

I glanced at my watch and decided that I had a good chunk of time before Cornelius was ready. I followed the signs to the outside, and was hit by the warmth of the Mexican sunshine.

Directly in front of me was the largest of the swimming pools. I knew it was the largest because I had read the hotel's guide book, left inside the suite. My head was full of useless pieces of information about the size of the hotel's facilities.

But to see the pool area for myself, up close, was incredible.

Almost an hour later, I peeled myself from the sun lounger and reluctantly headed back into the hotel's opulence.

I had found a lounger positioned so that my feet were in the shallow depths of the pool and my body faced the pool and the sea beyond it. The sun beamed down and kissed my skin with its rays, but my feet in the pool stopped the heat becoming overpowering.

After drying off, which magically only required me to hold my feet out of the water and in the sun's rays for a few seconds, I weaved my way through the happy mass of tourists and found that I reached the reception area just as the lift doors opened and Uncle Cornelius burst out, a grin upon his face.

"You found it!" I exclaimed, as I recognised the bright flamingo shirt.

"Funny story, actually," Cornelius said, his booming voice causing several people nearby to startle. "I knew I had it somewhere, lassie, it was just a case of recounting my steps. After you left the room, I spent some time drawing myself a mental map of the situation, as it is. I packed the whole of my suitcase again, that was the key!"

"You packed?"

Uncle Cornelius nodded furiously. "I rolled everything up, folded up the shirts nicely. Managed to get the whole lot back into the case, which is something to boast about, let me tell you! Then I dressed exactly as I had for the check in, and came down to reception with my case. I left the hotel, stood outside for a few moments, then arrived as if I'd never been here before. The receptionist was marvellous, I tell you, simply marvellous! They pretended to check me in, helped me up to the room, and left me there. Now, at this point I wondered if the plan would fail because, of course, when I checked in for real, you were with me. But fortune favours the brave, so I kept the faith and my stiff upper lip saw the way to victory!"

I must have worn my complete confusion on my face because Uncle Cornelius took one look at me and burst into laughter.

"It's okay, not everyone can have a mind like mine. The key is, Emily, if you need to find something, you have to look for it in the place where it is. But you don't know where that place is. Except, by repacking the case, I inadvertently returned it to that place and then discovered it. Makes sense?"

"Yes," I said, although I was sure of no such thing and was beginning to feel a little dizzy, perhaps from the sun or hunger but equally as likely to be because my uncle had just frazzled my brain.

"Shall we eat?"

"Yes!" I exclaimed eagerly.

"There's no time for a pre-dinner snack now, I'm afraid. In fact, we're a few minutes late for the chef's table, but they won't mind. And don't you feel guilty for putting us behind schedule, Emily, this is your holiday and you shouldn't feel under pressure to be on time for everything."

I raised my eyebrows at the suggestion that I was the one making us late, but said nothing. Cornelius may have an intricate system for discovering his lost clothes, but he had no idea how to be punctual. It was often as if the man was on a different time continuum completely.

"Follow me!" He commanded, and I did. We walked across the grand reception area, towards a dark doorway. A glass sign fixed to the wall told me that we had reached Mex, but nothing more than that one word.

Cornelius pushed open the door and we entered what was the most elegant restaurant I'd ever seen in my life. Darkly lit, with air conditioning so strong it could have convinced me we were back home in England, I noticed the places that were set included four pairs of knives and forks by each plate, and felt myself grow excited.

Whatever Mex specialised in, the evening promised to be a culinary delight.

"Ah, Cornelius!" A small man with a large, angry looking nose rushed forward and greeted my uncle with a hand shake and air kisses before turning his attentions to me.

"My niece, Emily," Cornelius introduced.

"Ah, such a pretty lady! How marvellous to meet you!"

"She apologises for putting us a few minutes behind schedule," Uncle C said with a wide, pleasant smile.

"No trouble at all. Please, follow me," he led us across to a large round table covered in a white cloth and laid in the same way as the other tables I had noticed. To my surprise, the table was full apart from the two empty seats that I guessed were for us, and at the head of the table was LuAnn from the lift.

"Cornelius, Emily, I presume you are familiar with the Cunninghams?"

The family at the table did look vaguely familiar, but I couldn't place how I could possibly know them or where from. They all looked as immaculate as LuAnn with their glossy hair, symmetrical features and perfect tans.

"The Cunningham family are here with us filming the season finale and have a very busy schedule, but tonight they asked for the chef's table and I know that Cornelius, you are always happy to accommodate."

"Of course! Every stranger is a friend I haven't had chance to talk to yet," Cornelius offered a wink.

LuAnn gave us a brief smile, then said, "Patrick, please do stop referring to this as the season finale. This is my daughter's wedding. The cameras are simply background chatter."

And then it came to me. Of course. We were sharing a table with *the* Cunningham family, from the incredibly successful reality show, *Keeping up With The Cunninghams!*

I glanced across the table quickly and sure enough, names came to me. LuAnn was the matriarch, the momager, who controlled every aspect of her three daughters' lives to precision. And there they were; bombshell oldest daughter Yasmine; the bride-to-be and cosmetic company owner Hattie; and the youngest, studious Damson who had her sights set on a law degree from Cambridge.

It was entirely impossible that I was going to share a meal, share a table, with these reality TV royalty, but even as I had that thought, I felt my treacherous arm raise to allow me to give an awkward wave, and my unbelievable mouth curve into a smile.

"So sorry for crashing your table, darlings. Do you mind awfully? We're simply dreadful, aren't we?" LuAnn asked as she leaned in and air kissed Cornelius, who seemed for once to be speechless.

"We don't mind at all," I said, because someone had to answer and really, how could anyone mind this happening? I couldn't imagine there was a table in the whole of the world where these people wouldn't be immediately made welcome, where extra seats and more food and clean plates wouldn't be found instantly.

"Gosh, listen to your accents! You're Brits, huh? Don't even let Damson hear you!" Hattie exclaimed, her Los Angeles twang full of excitement.

Damson looked across at me and gave a wry smile. "Whereabouts are you from? Your accent's kind of... confused."

"Yes it is. I travelled around a lot as a kid," I explained. Mentioning my childhood made me think of my mum. I wondered what she would think of this, to her little girl all grown up and mixing with the stars. She'd probably deeply disapprove.

"We're huge fans," Cornelius had found his voice again as he took his seat.

"You're too kind," LuAnn batted the compliment away.

"Here for a wedding, you say?"

"My baby's getting married," LuAnn gestured across the table to Hattie, who grinned.

"I'm the baby, remember, mom," Damson said with a smile.

"Sure, sure. But you're married to the textbooks, dear. And this trip is all about your sister. Hattie's waited years to get her turn to walk down the aisle!"

"She's only twenty-two, mama," Yasmine said with a laugh.

"But I've had to watch you get married like a zillion times," Hattie said.

A flash of anger crossed Yasmine's face but was gone as quick as it came, and her expression rearranged itself into a wide grin, a splash of laughter, a wink cast in my direction.

"Well, congratulations," I offered, and raised my glass towards Hattie, even though my glass was empty and Hattie was looking down at her phone, not me.

"Are the cameras on right now?" Cornelius asked eagerly as he surveyed the private area that housed the chef's table.

LuAnn reached across and squeezed his arm. If a person made a noise when they fell in love, I swear I just heard it.

"Don't worry, darling. No cameras tonight. We do get some time off, thankfully. It's important that we get family time off screen."

"Talking of family time. Where is dad?" Yasmine asked.

LuAnn's brows furrowed for a millisecond. "You know what he's like. He'll be running late or some big deal will have landed in his lap that just can't wait."

"He'd better not miss the wedding. He's been to all of Yasmine's!" Hattie sulked.

"How many times have you been married, if I can ask?" Cornelius looked at Yasmine. She wore a skin tight bodysuit that fit so well it may have been sprayed on to her skin. Her skin itself was flawless, either naturally perfect or aided by a foundation that blended with her skin so perfectly the two became one. And her silky hair was secured in a high pony-tail that only increased how dramatic her features were.

Rumour had it that her career had begun with the sharing of some rather raunchy photographs that her boyfriend shared with a buddy who had contacts in the magazine world. The buddy was hooked, apparently, and Yasmine found herself being offered life-changing sums of money to model professionally. It turned out, the whole world was as obsessed with her as the buddy had been, and perhaps in a sign of her gratitude with the buddy, or her anger towards the boyfriend, the buddy quickly replaced the boyfriend and became her first husband.

Yasmine laughed. "Only twice. They say the third time's the charm and Skye's surely that. You follow the show? You've probably seen him."

"I don't get much time for TV, but I watch your show whenever I can," Cornelius said.

"I knew you were a man of fine taste!" LuAnn gushed.

"Ah, well, there's a funny story there. Back in 1997, I was offered a reality show of my own. Confessions with Cornelius, they wanted to call it. This was all with Channel 4, of course. They imagined I'd be some kind of agony uncle, helping people with their problems and that kind of thing."

I listened, open-mouthed in shock.

"You never told me this," I exclaimed.

Cornelius shrugged. "You never asked."

"I bet the camera loves you," LuAnn said.

"Mom, where is dad? Can you call him?" Hattie asked.

"Call him yourself, darling. Your phone's never out of your hand."

"They're all the same at that age. Apart from my Emily, she's not one for this modern technology," Cornelius said, and offered me an affectionate smile.

"You're lucky!" LuAnn shrieked, clearly thinking that Cornelius was my father.

"You've got the right idea," Yasmine told me.

"Smart girl. Joining social media is the worst thing I've ever done," Damson offered.

"Fine. I'll text him." Hattie said.

"Don't text him!" LuAnn, Yasmine and Damson all called in unison, then burst into laughter.

"He never reads his messages," LuAnn explained with a smile.

"Your husband, you mean?" I asked.

LuAnn laughed. "Heck, no. I told him to pack up his things a long time ago."

"They're divorced. But dad's coming to the wedding, with his new wife."

"And Becker! Don't forget Becker. Because Tracy can't go anywhere without him even though he's like 21," Hattie said.

"He's eighteen," Damson corrected.

"Alright, Your Honour," Hattie said with an eye roll.

"It's very impressive that you include his new wife in the celebrations," Cornelius said. "And I'm sure you have a fine young man by your side as well, LuAnn?"

Yasmine grinned, her teeth whiter than could possibly be natural. I felt tempted to reach for my sunglasses even though we were indoors.

"Mother's far too dedicated to us three to make room in her life for a man," she said.

"Ah," Cornelius said.

"Anyway, enough about us! We're a hot mess. You two must have some fascinating tales to tell," LuAnn's eyes twinkled as she looked at Cornelius, then me.

It was clear to see how this family had become reality TV royalty. They were gracious, down to earth, and incredibly charming.

There was no way in the world that me and my uncle were the people the Cunninghams most wanted to be with right then, but that was how they made us feel. They were bright lights, and I felt myself begin to bask in their glory and attention.

It was a dangerous thing, however, asking Cornelius about the tales he could tell, and I busied myself with looking at the menu as he began to speak. Nobody else had even picked up the menu, which was on a long, thin piece of embossed card that was headed with my name and would clearly therefore have to be discarded after the single use.

Everything sounded good, even the dishes I was unfamiliar with. What was samphire? Would I like wagyu beef? I'd heard of foie gras but couldn't remember what it was. How could I ever choose?

Luckily, I didn't have to, as silent waiters appeared by the table and began to place small plates of food in front of us.

Damson must have noticed my confusion, because she met my gaze and whispered, "It's a tasting menu tonight. We get one of everything. Luckily, the portions are tiny!"

"Oh, wow," I murmured.

Cornelius continued to talk, the Cunninghams continued to play the role of a lively audience, and the food continued to appear.

As the night wore on, however, LuAnn became more agitated. Her glances at her diamond encrusted Patek Philippe became more frequent, and she began to drum her coffin-shaped nails on the tablecloth.

3

"I'm going to have to call your father. Excuse me," LuAnn said eventually, and the second she moved, a waiter was behind her, pulling her chair out so she didn't have to trouble herself. She glided out of the restaurant with a smile fixed to her face as people greeted her.

"I don't know why she can't just relax. We all know what dad's like," Yasmine said once she had gone.

"He's never been late for any of your weddings!" Hattie exclaimed.

"That's because we all flew together. I told you to make sure he arrived with us. As soon as mom isn't organising him, he falls apart."

"And Tracy won't be too invested in protecting my perfect wedding."

"Tracy's fine. She just doesn't mother him the way mom did," Damson said.

"Tracy's fine? Have you forgot that she broke up our family?" Yasmine asked.

"Oh, that was all dad. He told her he was single!"

"I'm sure everything will work out, girls. They normally do," Cornelius offered. The three Cunningham daughters turned, as one, and fixed him with smiles, smaller than the ones I suspected were for show. Genuine smiles. The Cunninghams were developing a soft spot for Uncle C.

"You're so lucky," Yasmine told me, and I had to agree. I was indeed.

Uncle Cornelius may be brash and constantly running late, and I suspected he had a blurred line when it came to telling the truth sometimes, but he was a good man with a heart of gold. I was lucky to have him in my life and to be on this trip with him.

LuAnn returned to the table and the energy around the table shifted slightly as each of us picked up on her change in mood.

"He doesn't think he can be here," she said, her tone scarily mild.

"Tonight? That's not such a big deal," Yasmine said.

"For the wedding. Your father doesn't think he can be here for the wedding, Hattie. I'm so sorry."

Hattie dropped her fork with a clang and a waiter dashed over, noticed the tone at the table, and retreated back to the shadows.

"This is a joke, right?"

"I wish it was."

"Well, what's his excuse?"

"Some contract he has to finalise. He sends his apologies."

"Oh, well, that's okay then! If he sends his apologies! I can't believe this is happening. You know, I joke that Yasmine's the favourite, but she really is. She gets married every year and he's always there! It's never an issue finding the time then! But here I am, about to have the only wedding I'll ever have in this lifetime, and his work is more important."

"Hey, don't turn this into being about me and you. This is all on dad," Yasmine said.

"She's right," LuAnn agreed.

"So I'm walking down the aisle on my own? No way. No, I can't do that. I'll have to cancel the whole thing!"

LuAnn let out a sigh, then picked up her wine glass and took a long sip. She gestured to the waiter. "I'm gonna need some more of this, ASAP."

"It seems an awful shame to cancel a whole wedding because of one person," Cornelius said.

"I agree. You've got the rest of your family here. Sometimes it isn't possible to have everyone present," I said. My voice caught, and the Cunninghams noticed and turned their attention to me.

"Sorry. I just thought... I lost my mum years ago. If I ever get married, I'll only have one parent there."

The Cunninghams glanced between me and Cornelius, clearly thinking he was the lone parent I meant, and I didn't correct them because my dad answered my calls so infrequently, part of me doubted whether he would even turn out on my big day.

"You are a good man," LuAnn reached out and squeezed Cornelius' hand again. She was beginning to slur her words.

"I try, ma'am," Cornelius said with a flourish as another plate of mysterious food appeared in front of us as if by magic.

"Actually," LuAnn said, then gasped and covered her mouth with her hand, her perfect nails almost stabbing her nostrils.

"What?" Cornelius asked.

"No, nothing, I couldn't," LuAnn glanced across at Yasmine, who met her gaze and shrugged.

"It's not a crazy idea," the eldest daughter said.

Cornelius gave a nervous chuckle.

4

Whatever idea LuAnn had had, she hadn't shared it yet.

Instead, she had insisted that Cornelius and I meet the rest of the family, who turned out to be the groom-to-be, Rafe, and Yasmine's latest beau, Skye, who met us at a private bar within the Mex restaurant.

"Here's my beautiful bride!" Rafe shouted as soon as we filed in, and he scooped Hattie up as if she was a doll and twirled her around in his arms. She squealed in a way that suggested she disapproved, but grinned in a way that suggested she very much approved.

"Knock it off, the cameras aren't even here," Damson said with a scowl.

Rafe glanced around, eyed me and Cornelius with suspicion, then lowered Hattie to the ground and returned to the bar, where he sat on a stool next to none other than Skye Portillo, son of a billionaire media mogul and something of a celebrity playboy. I was no slave to the rumour mill, but even I recognised his chiselled features and felt a little woozy being so close to him.

"Look at this place, lassie. We're travelling in style now!" Cornelius exclaimed, as if the rest of the hotel had been a slum until the Cunninghams had shown us this part.

"We really are," I agreed. The whole thing was surreal, and I knew that when I woke up the next morning, I'd wonder if any of it had actually happened.

"Drinks, ladies?" Cornelius offered.

LuAnn fluttered her eyelashes, apparently overcome with gratitude. As if this family was ever short of offers of drinks, food, space at the table, private airplanes, or anything else their hearts desired. And yet, she seemed so genuine. If star power was a person, it was LuAnn Cunningham.

"We'll all have water, thank you darling. We need clear heads!"

The daughters groaned, but didn't argue the point. The momager had spoken, and her word was final.

"You heard the fine lady. Water for everyone!" Cornelius declared as he approached the bar. The bar man, a thin man who looked to be around 70 years old, nodded and set up glasses for everyone.

"That'll be seventy dollars," he said.

Cornelius let out a laugh, but the bar man didn't appear to be joking.

"The Cunninghams only drink Evitali water, sir. Your bill is seventy dollars."

Cornelius' cheeks flushed and he stammered with what to say.

"Is everything okay here, darling? You really are too generous!" LuAnn said, as she picked up the glasses and began to distribute them among her family with stern orders that they should hydrate.

"Everything's grand. This man seems to imagine I carry

cash! Ha! Bill it to the Opal Suite, there's a good man," Cornelius said with a smile and a wiggle of his eyebrows.

"You're in the Opal Suite?" Skye Portillo turned and looked first at Cornelius, and then at me. His attention felt like the heat of a thousand suns, and I felt my jaw gape open and my head dumbly nod. Whatever words were, they had deserted me for the moment.

"We were there last year. Cool," Rafe said. He also turned and gave me a dazzling smile, and I reached for a bar stool before I fainted.

"Sorry, my manners are awful when I'm jetlagged. And I'm always jetlagged! Skye Portillo. And you are?"

"I'm Emily, and this is my erm... this is Cornelius," I said.

"Cool, cool. LuAnn got you guys talking and you couldn't escape?" Rafe gave me a meaningful look and a raised eyebrow.

I laughed. "No, nothing like that. We shared the chef's table and she just suggested we come along and meet you two."

"Thank you, LuAnn," Skye said and offered me a wink.

"Emily here is quite the catch," Cornelius said. I stared at him, hoping my gaze would burn into him and stop him talking, but no such luck. "She's a single lady, footloose and fancy free. Just playing the field."

Skye looked up at me through long lashes and cocked me a grin. That was it. I was in love. I shook my head and reminded myself that he was in a relationship. A relationship with Yasmine Cunningham! Not to mention the fact that he must have different women throwing themselves at him every day, and could surely do better than little old me.

Playing the field, indeed! I wouldn't know the first thing about playing the field!

"And how about you, Cornelius? Do you have a lady waiting for you back at home?" LuAnn appeared by our side again.

"Me? Well, actually, right now, you could say I'm in between options..."

"How lucky we are. Don't you think, gentlemen?"

"Sure," Rafe said.

"I can't believe my luck," Skye purred, his gaze still fixed on me.

"Skye, behave," LuAnn admonished.

"My sparkling personality's getting me in trouble again. Time for a visit to the little boys' room," he said, then walked away towards the toilet.

"He's harmless, but I'll warn you anyway. Stay away. I certainly wish my daughter had."

"You don't like him?" I asked in disbelief. How anyone could be impervious to his charms was beyond my comprehension.

"Oh, I like him fine as a person. I'd love him as a son, no doubt. But as the holder of my daughter's heart? No way. I still hope that Yasmine will come to her senses one day and reconcile with her ex."

"With Derrick?"

LuAnn pulled a face. "No, not him. He saw Yasmine as a product to be marketed and sold, and he made darn sure he got a good cut of everything. I mean her second husband, Wayne."

I flushed. "I don't really follow the news, sorry. I don't know about him."

"Oh! He was a breath of fresh air! A dog walker. They met when he started walking her chihuahua, Dior."

"That's cute," I said. I had heard about Dior, and I

wondered if it was meaningful that more news about the dog than the husband had reached my ears. That chihuahua had a wardrobe of tailor made clothes that was worth more than the whole of my personal belongings.

In fact, I was surprised that she hadn't brought the pet with her.

"You two are getting on well, I see," Cornelius interrupted. He was clearly as entranced by LuAnn as I was by Skye.

"Oh, Cornelius. Can I just come out and ask you something? A favour? I know it's horrendously cheeky, but life's too short!"

"Ask away," Cornelius said, with a waggle of his monobrow.

"You've heard that we've been awfully let down. Well, Hattie's been awfully let down. Her father is a wonderful man if you're one of his clients! But these girls have been stuck getting the leftover pieces of his time for too long. I can't stand that Hattie will be let down on her big day!"

"It is awful," Cornelius agreed.

"And she's not like Yasmine. She won't stay married for a month or two and then move on to the next. There's a real chance that she'll stay married to Rafe for... well... a long time, maybe."

"Good for her," Cornelius said.

"Here's my idea. Maybe it is crazy! But you seem like such an awfully nice man, and I know you'd never let your daughter marry without you being there. I was wondering, do you think you'd do the honour?"

"His daughter?" I asked.

"The honour?" Cornelius asked.

"Would you walk Hattie down the aisle?" LuAnn asked.

"Wow," I murmured. LuAnn was right, it was a crazy idea, and yet in the moment it felt like a perfectly reasonable suggestion. The father of the groom was absent. What else was there to do?

"The honour would be all mine," Cornelius said, and with a bow he leaned over and kissed LuAnn's hand.

"Great! Oh, this is marvellous! We need to get the cameras in here. You're okay with cameras, right? The whole world is going to watch this wedding."

Cornelius grinned and my stomach flipped. I'd never been a person who had dreamed of fame and celebrity, but I could see that the idea was absolutely fine with my uncle.

"Do you want to think about it?" I whispered in his ear.

"A moment, please?" Cornelius told LuAnn, and stepped away with me towards an empty table. Immediately, a waiter was by our side, cocktail drink in hand, and Cornelius batted him away with a swift shake of his head.

"It's a lovely gesture," I began.

"Ah, well, there's no choice really, is there! What am I meant to do, say no and leave the poor girl high and dry without an arm to give her away?"

"Well, no. When you put it like that, of course you should help where you can," I agreed.

"What is it then, lassie?"

"I just... a wedding is so personal. And we're strangers to these people! They move in a whole different world to us," I tried to explain my reservations.

"That doesn't make them better than us, you know," Uncle C said.

"I know!"

"You know, Emily, some of the best things in life have come to me when I've said yes to an adventure."

"Really?" I asked.

Cornelius draped a heavy arm around my shoulders. "There was this one time, when a young girl rang me up. Completely out of the blue. Asked if she could come to meet me."

I felt my cheeks flame. "Well, that was..."

"Terrifying!" Cornelius finished my sentence.

"No, it was not!" I argued.

"Trust me, lassie, it was. I had no idea what your mother had told you about me. I knew her opinion of me was so low it had stopped her ever letting me meet you. You could have been calling to scold me for any number of wrongs I couldn't even begin to imagine! So, I had a choice. I stayed safe and said I couldn't meet. Or I said yes to the unknown."

"I'm glad you said yes," I admitted.

"Me too, Emily. Me too," Cornelius said as he pulled me into a hug. It was like being enveloped in the arms of a bear, and I allowed myself to snuggle into his warmth and protection.

"You should give Hattie away. Of course you should."

"You're sure?"

I pulled away and nodded. "Yes. You're a man who does the right thing, and this is the right thing."

"LuAnn, darling, the wedding's on!" Cornelius called across the room.

LuAnn turned, met his gaze, and punched the air in celebration.

As she did, the doors to the private bar opened, and a stream of funky looking young men and women streamed in, cameras on their shoulders.

"Ready?" The man who looked slightly older than the others addressed LuAnn, and as soon as she gave the slightest nod of her head, he turned to the rest of the crew and hollered, "Action!"

"I guess the decision's made," I murmured, and adopted what I hoped was my biggest smile.

"Hey, pretty lady. Care for a drink?" My thoughts were interrupted by none other than Skye Portillo.

"Just a tap water, please," I said. Keeping a clear head seemed like the smartest decision I could make when my whole life appeared to be completely out of control.

"Tap water? That's like, so, cool. This is going to be epic, you know? Maximilian's going to freak when he hears about it!"

"Who's Maximilian?"

Skye's eyes opened wide with admiration. "You really are the coolest chick. Yeah! Who's Maximilian? That's what I'm saying!"

"No, I mean I really don't know who he is," I admitted.

"Oh. Seriously? Wow... well, he's LuAnn's ex."

"Oh! The father of the bride. You think he'll be annoyed that Cornelius has taken his place? On the wedding day, I mean. I'm not suggesting anyone thinks he's her new dad."

Skye laughed and his eyes twinkled. "He's going to lose his mind anyway when he sees what I'm planning."

"Oh," I said. I wished I had the confidence to ask what he was planning, but I'd been brought up to disdain nosiness. If he wanted me to know, he'd tell me.

To my delight and horror, he leaned in close as if he was going to kiss me, but then whispered in my ear. "I'm going to propose to Yasmine."

"You are? Wow, that's amazing."

"Right? I was going to do it tomorrow, at the wedding rehearsal, but I might just do it tonight. Now the cameras are back, what's the point in waiting?"

"Why do the cameras matter?" I asked.

Skye laughed again. "Can you imagine what the press is going to make of Yasmine's third engagement? Everyone's been saying she's still hung up on that moron Wayne because we've been together for six months without any wedding bells. But we're just taking it slow."

"Well, six months doesn't seem that long before proposing. Won't Hattie be annoyed about the timing?"

"Of course she will! But she's always been the B-lister. The show's only relevant because of Yasmine and this whole season has been Hattie this, Hattie that. It's freaking dull, man! Look, it's my idea and everything, but let's just say the network won't be disappointed."

"They know?!" I exclaimed.

Skye shrugged. "Might even have been their idea. Of course, as soon as I heard it, I knew it was genius. Let them end the penultimate episode with the proposal, and then the whole world tunes in for the finale, but not for Hattie and Rafe, for me and Yasmine! It's probably going to be the highest ratings the network has ever had."

"And Yasmine doesn't know?" I asked. I was finding it hard to keep track of what was real life or real love, and what was being orchestrated by the network for their ratings.

"Nah, call me an old romantic. I want her to be surprised when I pop the question," Skye said, with a wink.

"That's really sweet," I said, although I wasn't so sure that a public proposal just as my sister was about to get married was something I'd want. Luckily, I didn't have a sister. Or a TV show. Or a boyfriend. Yeah, I guess there was no chance of me ending up in the same position.

"We should hang out later," Skye murmured, and he reached across to me, took a loose tendril of hair in between his lean fingers, twirled it, then tucked it neatly behind my ear.

Luckily, I couldn't breathe, which was helpful because I didn't know how to possibly answer that suggestion. We'd already had dinner, a whole tasting menu of culinary sensations, and were now in a private bar, and Skye Portillo was making plans for later? With me?

"Skye?"

His hand jumped away from my face and I felt my cheeks flush as Yasmine glared at us.

I was pretty sure I'd done nothing wrong, only had my hair touched without my request, and yet I still gazed at the floor like a child being scolded.

"Here she is, my better half," Skye opened his arms wide and attempted to pull Yasmine to him, but she refused to move. Rumour had it, she had an impressive martial arts history, and right then she looked very much like a woman not to be messed with.

"What are you doing?" She hissed.

"Working the room, making new friends," Skye grinned.

"You've got more than enough female friends," Yasmine said.

Skye opened his eyes wide and clutched his hand to his chest. "Yasmine Cunningham, you insult me with your suspicious mind!"

She tutted and turned her attentions to me. "Look, Emily, it's super nice what your dad's doing for Hattie. And you seem like a nice girl. But you can't possibly understand the kind of man Skye is."

"We were just chatting," I said.

"Oh, I'm sure you were just chatting. I'm sure you're a fan of girl power and female friendship, and all standing together in unison. I'm sure you have good morals and your head would never be turned. Not by a handsome, rich man, and not by the chance to play up your part on a TV show."

"I..."

"But Skye? He's been working the women and the cameras for as long as he's been alive. He doesn't even know it's happening. He can't switch it off. So, Emily, I'm telling you to be very careful."

"Of course," I agreed.

She looked me up and down and leaned in close. "I will not have another relationship fail. You understand me? Oh, and we're going to have to lend you an outfit for the wedding."

"That's... of course... thank you," I spluttered.

When Yasmine turned, all of the cameras were focused on her, because Skye Portillo was behind her, on one knee. In his open hand was a ring box, and inside was the grandest diamond ring I had ever seen in my life.

"Yasmine Cunningham, you make everything better. Will you do me the honour of being my wife?" Skye flashed her a grin.

Despite her beauty, wealth and fame, Yasmine transformed into a puddle of romantic dreams as she realised what was happening.

"Are you kidding me? You're doing this right now?" Hattie exclaimed as she stomped across. The cameras spanned to include her in their footage.

"Skye, man, what the heck?" Rafe was by her side, his jaw tight with fury.

"Yes! Yes! Of course I will!" Yasmine squealed, and Skye jumped to his feet and picked her up from the floor, twirled her around and around. As he set her down, he grinned across at the cameras, then turned and winked at me.

"How can you be so selfish?" Hattie asked.

"Hattie, not now," LuAnn said.

"I can't believe I'm going to be Mrs Skye Portillo! Have you seen this ring?" Yasmine cooed as she held out her hand. The diamonds twinkled in a hypnotic way.

"We're here for a wedding, Yasmine, but this time it's not yours! You know what? You're so sad. You can't stand the attention being on me for once, can you?"

"Hattie? What do you mean? I had no idea Skye was going to propose," Yasmine said.

"Yeah, right! Of course you knew. You control everything!"

"Hattie, come on. We don't need this. We're getting married for ourselves, not for them or anyone else. Let's go," Rafe said.

Hattie bit her lip and eyed her sister, clearly desperate to say more.

"Go on, Hattie. Don't ruin the night," Damson suggested.

"What do you know about love?" Hattie spat at her younger sister.

"This argument doesn't seem to be about love. It seems to be about attention and the TV show and your egos! Love isn't for show. It's meant to be sacred and private."

Everyone turned to look at Damson, the quiet one. Her words were powerful, but even more so coming from her. She was the sister who refused interviews because of her study timetable and had publicly denounced the idea of celebrity as a career choice.

"Wise words, sis," Yasmine said, but her attention was still caught up in admiring the diamond ring.

"Let's get out of here," Hattie huffed, and she grabbed hold of Rafe's hand and led him out of the bar and back through the restaurant.

Yasmine raised her eyebrows and shrugged at the rest of us.

"You know, my services are available if you also need a father of the bride stand in," Cornelius exclaimed with a wiggle of his eyebrows, and our laughter must have carried across the space for Hattie to hear.

5

B eing adopted into the Cunningham wedding party transformed the relaxing break that Cornelius and I had been expecting.

Gone was the lie in we had been looking forward to, and instead we were awoken not by an alarm clock but by the hammering on our door by a member of staff, paid and given the responsibility to ensure that we didn't oversleep for a moment.

"Okay, we're up!" I groaned, but the knocking persisted.

I peeled my eyes open and saw that it was still dark, the room illuminated only by the light from the moon as it reflected upon the night sea.

I glanced at the clock; it was just after 2am. A horrendous time to be awake. Not that Uncle Cornelius could share me in my displeasure; I could hear his snoring coming from the next room.

The hammering continued, and I realised it was a more urgent, aggressive knocking than the staff would inflict on a paying guest. Well, a guest. I couldn't say I was 100% certain that we were paying guests. Cornelius seemed to have a knack for travelling in a way that didn't empty his wallet.

I jumped out of bed, grabbed the closest thing that could be a weapon if needed, and padded lightly across to the door of the suite, which I pulled open slowly.

In front of me was Yasmine Cunningham, dressed in baby pink silk pyjamas, her hair draped loose across her shoulders, her face somehow even more attractive free of make-up. She looked younger, and less worldly wise; like the Yasmine she would have no doubt become without any celebrity status.

"Yasmine! Is everything okay?" I asked.

I noticed how jittery she was, treading from one foot to the other as if the floor was burning coals and her skin could only stand the heat for a moment.

"What are you doing with a cucumber?"

I glanced at the long, slim item that I'd picked up in the dark and, unable to think of any reasonable excuse, grinned maniacally.

"Can I come in?"

"Sure," I said, and held the door open. To my amazement, she led the way right into my bedroom and collapsed into the bed, even pulling the sheets over her. Tucked into bed like that, there was something childlike about her.

"Shall I make us a cup of tea?" I asked.

She gave a weak laugh. "You really are British. They say that you guys cure everything with endless mugs of tea. Sure, I'll give it a try. It can't make things worse."

I filled the kettle and considered the hotel's selection of fancy teas, but I knew that in a time of crisis, there was really nothing better than good old PG Tips. Luckily, Cornelius never left home without an emergency supply, which I raided in good conscience because whatever the situation was, it was a definite crisis.

Two mugs of steaming tea ready, I returned to the bedroom and placed one on each bedside table, then climbed into bed next to Yasmine.

"You don't have to talk about it," I said.

"Oh, I need to talk about it. And right now, I can't speak to my family."

"Hattie will calm down," I said.

Yasmine scoffed. "Of course she will. I'm not worried about her."

"Oh. Has something else happened?"

"Yes! Something else has happened! One of them has betrayed me."

"Really?" I asked.

Yasmine nodded, picked up the mug, and took a sip of the tea. "Mm, this is good. Maybe you English have the right idea. It's very civilised. Make a mug of tea and sort things out with a stiff upper lip. Oh, who am I kidding? I just don't know what to do, Emily."

"I'm sure it will all work out," I soothed. My life experience was so minimal that I was fairly confident whatever Yasmine was going through, it would be well out of my comfort zone. But if a mug of tea and a safe retreat into my bed helped at all, I was happy to play my part.

"Have you ever been madly in love?" She asked.

I felt my cheeks flush as my mind immediately pictured Skye, but that wasn't love. Nowhere near. He was just a handsome guy who had paid me a little attention. I shook my head.

"Take my advice, don't. It's nothing but pain and misery."

"Has something happened with Skye?" I asked. I

suddenly felt nervous. What if Yasmine had come to my room under false pretences and was about to tell me to back off and leave Skye alone?

Yasmine shrugged. "Maybe, maybe not. I'm not talking about him. There's only been one man for me, apart from daddy."

"Oh," I said, utterly confused.

"You never met Wayne," she said, as if we hadn't just met that day. I hadn't met 99% of the people in her life, and no doubt never would. I was under no illusions that Yasmine Cunningham and I were suddenly BFFs. No, we were having a platonic version of a holiday romance. I was available, even in the middle of the night, for a brief period of time when she was choosing not to open up to her family and had nobody else available.

And yet. It was still flattering to be the target of her attention, even temporarily. Even as a last - or only - option.

"You'd love him. He's so down to earth. Doesn't care about this nonsense at all," Yasmine said with a nostalgic smile.

"What happened?"

"Oh, I ruined it. Of course."

I didn't quite know what to say to that, so I took a sip of my own tea and sat in companionable silence with her. It struck me for a second that I may not be the last option for Yasmine to speak to. She may be a woman who had everything, apart from genuine friends.

"Everything seems worse during the night. That's what my mum used to tell me," I said.

Yasmine reached out and took my hand, gave it a squeeze. "Oh, it's going to seem much worse in the morning."

"It is?"

"Yep."

"You can't be sure of that. It might feel like that now, but that's the night time talking."

"No, it really is going to get worse tomorrow."

"How come?"

"He's here."

"Who?"

"Wayne. He's at the hotel. One of those snakes who call themselves my family must have called him, got him on the first flight down here."

"Maybe that's a good thing?"

Yasmine looked at me, her brown eyes huge and longing with hope. "You really think it could be?"

"Well, if he's the only man you've ever loved, surely seeing him again can't be a bad thing."

Yasmine laughed. "Oh, of course it can! Just because I loved him doesn't mean we're going to have a happy ever after. This isn't TV, you know."

I raised an eyebrow.

"Well, you know what I mean. This is still my life. Skye will take one look at Wayne and... and..."

"And what?" I asked. My stomach flipped as I imagined the four of us on an uncomplicated double date, laughing about how the universe had helped us arrange into our correct couplings. Skye and I. Yasmine and Wayne.

"He's very possessive. He'll flip when he sees Wayne."

"Oh. Of course. He doesn't seem possessive."

"The unfaithful ones always are. You'll learn. Or hopefully not."

"Yasmine, has Skye cheated on you?"

"Of course he has. He's incapable of staying loyal to anything other than his ego."

"Why do you stay with him?" I asked. I couldn't imagine

the pain of knowing the man I loved was cheating on me. Whatever the media might say about Yasmine, she had sure had a series of bad luck when it came to men.

Yasmine sighed. "I'm just having some fun with him. Plus, after Wayne, the media crucified me. It makes a nice change to have the public feeling sorry for me for a change. I'll break it off before the wedding. Maybe even leave him at the altar?"

"You already know you won't marry him but you accepted his proposal?"

"Look, Emily, this work is a different world than most people can understand. I'm employed by a television company to get them good ratings. As soon as I stop doing that, the series is gone. And yes, my family are on the show, but I'm the big name. I know the timing of the proposal looks bad, but everything I do is focused on making sure we're all still relevant."

"That makes sense," I said. It really did. Yasmine was in a position where she had to consider her every lifestyle choice and relationship as a business deal. It wasn't a position I'd like to be in, and I wondered how much her fame had contributed to her losing the love of her life.

"Thank you for listening to me," she said with a yawn.

"Anytime. What do you think you'll do tomorrow, when you see Wayne?"

"Oh, the usual. Collapse like a puddle at his feet," she said, her voice groggy. As she spoke, she snuggled down and closed her eyes, and a second later the change in her breathing indicated that she was fast asleep.

I lay down on the other side of the bed and closed my eyes, but my mind raced with a million thoughts, an embarrassing amount of them about Skye Portillo.

6

I woke the next morning at 4.30am, my head thick and
confused by what had been a dream and what hadn't.
The other side of the bed was empty, but the empty
mug of tea was evidence that my night time visitor had been
real.

I needed fresh air.

I showered, dressed quickly in a polka dot sundress, and
slipped out of the suite. Cornelius' snores confirmed that he
was still firmly in dream land.

At reception, a man I vaguely recognised was checking
in, loudly and with aggression. I paused by the lifts to study
him for a moment as he argued with the receptionist.

"No, I don't have a room reserved. Do I look like a man
who books his own rooms? I'll stay in the Opal. What do
you mean it's reserved? I always stay there!"

I grimaced and rushed away. He was clearly an important person, at least in his own head. Why was his face
familiar?

I hadn't got far out of the doors and into the baking sun

before I saw Damson spread out on a sun lounger, a text-book in her hands. She waved me over.

"You're escaping Derrick too?"

"Derrick?" I asked.

She rolled her eyes. "He was kicking up a storm at reception when I came down. I managed to get out here without him noticing. Assumed you'd done the same."

"There was a man arguing at reception and he looked familiar, but I don't think I know him."

"You'll know of him. Derrick Riches. Yasmine's first ex-husband."

"Yes! That's him! Hold on... Derrick is here?" I spluttered. Yasmine had told me last night that Wayne was here. Wayne. Not Derrick. Or had I misremembered?

"Clearly someone thinks that Hattie's wedding isn't going to do enough for the ratings on its own," Damson said with a sigh.

"Wow," I said.

Damson laughed. "That sums it up pretty well. Gosh, you must think we're all absolutely stark raving mad. Not that you'd be wrong."

"I think you're all lovely. But this is all a bit more intense than my life."

"Listen, Emily, if you ever get the chance to be famous beyond your wildest dreams, don't."

I gave a cocked smile. "I'm pretty sure I'd never get the chance, but thanks for the advice. You wish you weren't famous?"

"I'm not going to be famous. I'll disappear from public view as soon as I get across to England to study. That's when my real life will start."

"Sounds good, but you're already famous, aren't you?"

"Marginally. I'll be forgotten quickly. It is possible, you

know. Remember Ozzy Osbourne? His family had a reality show. His wife was on it, and his daughter Kelly and son Jack."

"That rings a bell," I said, although I had a childhood that didn't include much television watching.

"The thing that most people don't realise is, there's another daughter. Amy. She opted out of the show, didn't want to be part of it."

"You want to be like her," I murmured.

"It's going to be amazing. We'll be so happy without all of this madness."

I was about to ask who she meant by *we*, but we were interrupted.

"Damson! What the hell are you playing at?"

We turned to see Skye storming across the path towards us, his face glowering with fury. Behind him, a procession of cameras followed, focused not only on his warpath but on our reaction.

Somehow, I had managed to get myself right in the middle of another Cunningham family drama.

"Speaking of the devil," Damson shot me a wink.

"You can wipe that smug little smile off your face right now. Do you have any idea what you've done?"

"Good morning Skye, it's nice to see you too."

"Don't play smart with me. I've got a good idea to involve your father!"

"Please feel free to try. Nobody else has been able to reach him so far but good luck to you."

I watched in horror as Skye leaned in, pulled the textbook out of Damson's hands and waved it in the air.

"That's enough, Skye. Stop this right now!"

"Oh, I should stop it! I know you're the one who got Yasmine's exes here. You think you'll send us a message about true love, but you know nothing. You're just a little kid!"

"You think I wasted my time contacting Derrick and Wayne? I didn't like them when they were part of the family. Trust me, I have no desire to see them again."

"It had to be you! Hattie and Rafe wouldn't do anything to put their big day at risk, and that goes for LuAnn too. But you? You're so pathetic. You're jealous of Yasmine, and you should be! You're nothing like her!"

"I don't want to be anything like her. In case you haven't noticed, Skye, I'm my own person. Now give me back my book."

Skye sneered at her, threw his arm back, then tossed the textbook into the pool with all of his strength. The book landed in the middle of the clear water and began its soggy descent.

"Argh! How could you? You... you... argh!" Damson shrieked, and before he knew what was coming, she reared back and pushed him into the water.

He landed with a splash and Damson barged her way towards the camera team, her face like thunder. I jogged after her, apologising as I darted in between the cameras.

"Damson, are you okay?" I called as we returned to the inside of the hotel.

"I'll be fine. I just really needed that book. I'd better speak to the concierge and get another copy ordered."

"Of course. I'll, erm, see you later," I said, but Damson had already turned and left.

My stomach flipped as I considered what had just happened. It was barely 5am and there had already been more drama than I was used to in a whole year.

With a sad smile, I pushed the lift button and made my

way back upstairs to ensure that Cornelius was up and ready in time.

Only as I reached the Opal Suite did I realise that Skye had been wearing nothing but swimming trunks. Almost as if he'd been expecting to be pushed into the pool.

CORNELIUS EMERGED from his bedroom five minutes before we were due to meet the Cunninghams. He was draped in an expensive waffle towelling robe and looked as if he'd tossed and turned the whole night, which I knew by his snoring couldn't be the case.

"Are you okay?" I asked.

"Please tell me there's a mug of tea waiting with my name on," he groaned as he staggered out to the balcony. It was promising to be another beautiful day in Mexico, and holiday makers were already out reserving the best sun loungers and taking a dip in the pools.

"Oh, sure! I can make you one. We don't have much time, though."

Cornelius batted my concerns away and stood at the balcony railing. "I've never rushed around for a woman before and I don't intend to start now."

I grinned. "So, you've got your eye on LuAnn?"

"No, no, no. We're from completely different worlds. This isn't a romantic escapade, more of a... erm... good samaritan thing. Now that you've mentioned romance, though, Emily, don't think I haven't noticed that that young Skye has taken your eye!"

It was my turn to try to divert the topic. I decided the best way to do that was to ignore him completely and return inside to make tea.

Uncle Cornelius was amazing, but he had the attention span of a fruit fly and would soon be distracted from any interest in my non-existent love life.

Armed with two steaming cups, I was reminded of the nighttime visitor I'd had and curious as to whether Cornelius had heard anything.

"Did you sleep well?" I asked as I handed him one of the cups.

"Like the dead," he said with a laugh. "How about you? You're up and ready early."

"I've been up for a while," I admitted. I would tell him about Yasmine turning up, and about Damson and Skye arguing, but not when we were already running late.

Finally, he was convinced to drink up and get ready, and we made our way downstairs.

The wedding party had reserved an entire pool which was hidden from view away from the rest of the grounds and rooms.

A member of the hotel team guarded the entrance to the area but allowed Cornelius and I entry with a grin and a wiggle of his eyebrows.

The scene in front of us was beyond belief.

Cunninghams were draped across sun loungers, a DJ that I recognised from TV played a set in the corner, and a full bar service ensured that not a single drink was empty before its refill was provided. The cameras were discrete, but present, of course, and I tried to avoid staring right at them.

"Emily! Over here!" Yasmine called. She was on a lounger in a gold bikini, her tanned skin glistening with water droplets, no doubt from a recent dip in the pool.

I realised with a start that I was seeing Yasmine Cunningham in her natural habitat.

I gave her a little wave and sat awkwardly on the lounger next to her.

"How are you feeling today?" I asked.

She leaned in and narrowed her eyes. "Oh, I'm acting like everything's fine. I won't give them the satisfaction of seeing my pain."

"Who do you mean?"

"Whoever got Derrick and Wayne here! I don't know which one of them it was. Heck, maybe they're all in on it. And you know why? Because they don't think Hattie's wedding will be enough as a season finale. They're terrified that the family cash cow is going to stop giving them milk!"

I tried not to allow that visual to take root in my mind, and instead reached out and took Yasmine's hand in mine. "This is your family. I'm sure nobody's done anything deliberately to hurt you."

She let out a puff of air. "You don't know them, Emily. I know it sounds crazy, but you have to believe me. I know what they're capable of. Right now, you're the only person here that I trust!"

I was flattered, until I noticed that Yasmine cast a dramatic look out towards her family, and I realised that our whole conversation was being captured on film. Was I just a pawn in a storyline? I had no idea, but I did know there was at least a possibility that her words were genuine, and I couldn't stand the idea that she felt alone and betrayed by her nearest and dearest.

"I'll help you," I gave her hand a squeeze.

A figure walked by the far side of the pool and I saw Yasmine's eyes trail his every step.

"Is that him?" I asked.

"That's Wayne. The greatest man who ever walked the planet."

He seemed like a regular guy. In fact, he looked almost as out of place as Uncle C and I did, with his pale skin and supermarket flip flops.

"Still pining over your bit of rough, eh?" A sneering voice called out. Yasmine and I both turned to follow the sound and saw Derrick grinning at us from a nearby lounger.

"He was never my bit of rough," Yasmine protested.

Derrick cackled. "It's cute that you still have that fantasy of things working out with him, babe. Even after you screwed it up so royally, pardon the pun!"

"Be quiet, Derrick. What are you even doing here?"

"Part of the family, ain't I? I'd never miss Little Hat's wedding. Not everything's about you, you know."

"You never even got on with Hattie!"

"True, true. I found her dull as dish water if you really want my opinion. But, still. A wedding's a wedding... a chance for the whole family to get together."

Yasmine rolled her eyes and returned her attention to me. "Here's the first rule when it comes to Derrick Riches. Don't believe a word he says."

"Maybe he really is just here to celebrate the wedding. Is that really so unlikely?"

Yasmine scoffed. "Derrick's never celebrated another person's success or happiness. The absolute best reason he's here is to get his ugly mug back on TV, but he could be up to far worse than that."

"But surely him and Wayne are here for the same reason?" I said.

Yasmine exhaled, then stood up. Her lean legs seemed to go on forever. I watched as Wayne studied her perfect form from across the pool. Perhaps the regret about their break up was not one sided. But then he scowled and picked up a battered paperback, which he then lost himself in reading.

"I can't deal with this. Just promise me you'll stay close? I really could do with a friend."

"Of course. I'm right here. What's the plan for the day?"

"We have massages, a tai chi class, green smoothies for lunch, there's a walk on the private beach later, and karaoke tonight. So, not much really," Yasmine said with no hint of sarcasm. Clearly what passed for a busy day was very different for the two of us.

"That sounds really fun. I'll be with you every step of the way. I still can't believe Uncle C and I are part of all this. It's surreal."

"It's that alright. Listen, I need to speak to Wayne or the press will make a thing about what the silence between us means. Will you come over with me?"

"Of course," I agreed, and Yasmine lead the way.

We stood in front of his lounger and he lowered the book when he realised there was someone blocking the sun. When he saw that it was Yasmine, he smiled involuntarily, then reset his features and gave a mild nod towards her.

"Hey," Yasmine played with her hair as she greeted him.

"What's up?"

"Oh, everything's great. How are you doing? This is a... surprise. A nice one."

"Sure thing. I'm good."

"You've been keeping busy?"

Wayne shrugged. "Who's your friend?"

"Oh! This is Emily. Emily, this is Wayne."

"Pleased to meet you," I said.

"Likewise," Wayne closed his book and offered me his hand, which I shook lightly.

"When I noticed you over here, I was telling Emily it had

been so long since we'd seen each other. Isn't life weird like that?"

"No, life isn't weird at all, Yas. It's not like it's a surprise that we don't see each other. That's because you had sex with a Prince, Yasmine," Wayne deadpanned.

Yasmine's cheeks flushed and her eyes filled with tears.

"Hey, let's not do this now. We don't want anything to spoil Hattie's celebrations," I urged.

Wayne's shoulders dropped and the man appeared to deflate in front of me, like a balloon that had been popped. "You're right. Sorry. I debated whether to come and I thought I'd be fine. I guess I didn't realise how it would be to see you again. It just brings it all back."

"It does for me too. What we had was so special..."

"I don't mean it brings back the good times, Yas. It brings back the bad times. You broke my heart and I walked away without a word. I had to, I couldn't trust myself to say anything. And I'm not going to say things now," Wayne made moves to get up from the lounger.

"Wayne, please..."

"Emily here is right. This is Hattie's special occasion and I'm touched to be invited. I never even thought she liked me. I'll get myself composed, but it's probably best that we keep away from each other."

"Wayne..."

"I wish I was a bigger man, Yas. A better man even. Maybe another guy could stand here and wish you well, hope you have a great future with Skye Portillo even though the whole world knows he's screwing around behind your back. I can't do it. I can't send you off to another wedding that's not going to last. God, I can't even wish you unhappiness, Yas. He's not good enough for you. Even after everything you did to me, I care too darn much to stand by and see you with a guy who doesn't respect you. Ugh... look... I've said too much."

We watched in stunned silence as he trudged away from the lounger and sat at the bar, his back to everyone else.

"Well, Emily, there you have it. That's Wayne Jones for you. Looking out for me, even when he hates me."

"That man's a wet blanket!" Derrick shouted across at us.

Yasmine looked on the verge of tears, but there was no time for high emotions because a beautiful Mexican woman appeared and told us it was time for massages.

"Ooh, goodie!" Cornelius exclaimed. He would never part with his own money to splurge on a massage, but there was no end to the luxuries he could enjoy when someone else was footing the bill.

"I've never had a massage," I confided in him. My mother had thought self-care was a vanity of such a level it personally offended Jesus.

"You'll love it," Cornelius said.

"Do I have to get naked?" I asked.

LuAnn giggled and increased her pace so she fell into step with us. I watched in surprise as she linked her dainty, tanned arm through Cornelius'.

"You'll have privacy, don't worry. Have I mentioned that I really am so pleased to have met you both? Not to forget how grateful I am that you can fit this in your plans. You didn't have any sightseeing to do today?"

Cornelius gave a belly laugh. "We've just come from Dia de los Muertos over on Janitzio Island. We were looking forward to a few days to kick back and relax."

"Gosh! That sounds fascinating. Do you promise to tell me all about it, Corny?"

Corny? I said nothing and wondered if LuAnn knew

what she was getting herself into, asking him to make such a promise.

"Yes, yes, although I imagine you've seen more of the world than I have?"

"I doubt it. We do the index card version of travelling. We fly in, get transported to whichever hotel is deemed the easiest to manage our safety in, and then we fly out. Now, back when I was younger and the world had never heard of LuAnn Cunningham, I loved to travel. I spent a summer backpacking my way through Bali."

"Wow," I said. Bali was high on my own list of dream destinations. Something about the place looked so exotic.

"There are some good hotels out there. The Nusa Dua's my own favourite. You'll know it, I imagine?" Cornelius asked.

"I didn't know you'd been to Bali," I said.

"Work trip. Awfully dull."

LuAnn batted his arm and laughed. "When I say I backpacked, I mean it. I didn't have two dollars to rub together back then. Of course, the year after, Maximilian strode into my life and rescued me from poverty."

"He did?"

"No, I'm being facetious, dear. That's what he thought he was doing. My family were doing fine, but there was no way my parents would agree to me going to Bali. So I saved my candy striping wages and booked the flights. It turned out there wasn't much cash left after that, but really, with those beaches, who needs cash? I was in my element."

"Now that's the way to travel!" Cornelius enthused.

"I could have stayed forever."

"Why didn't you?" I asked. I knew that people did. Since Cornelius had guided me through his Facebook account (I still refused to have my own), I'd found two former school friends who had moved their lives across the world. Regular people packing their bags and starting new lives! I felt a shiver of thrill for them as I looked at photographs of them, sun drenched and happy.

The smile didn't leave LuAnn's face, but it appeared to freeze in place to disguise her true emotions. "There was an urgent situation at home. I had to cut the trip short and I never went back."

"I'm sorry," I said.

She shrugged, composure returned. "Look at all this, Emily. Look at my daughters."

Up ahead, the Mexican lady was guiding each of us into individual cabanas overlooking the beach.

"They're wonderful," I said.

In front of us, a man in a linen suit emerged from the hotel, trailed by a mousy woman who could have been staff as easily as a guest, and a teenage boy with floppy hair.

LuAnn let out a barely perceptible groan. "Emily, I can't regret a single thing in my life. Not even agreeing to marry *him*."

She gave Cornelius and me a smile, and then directed her attention on the man, who approached her with a wide grin.

"LuAnn, how wonderful to be here. What an occasion!"

"What on earth are you doing?" she hissed.

"LuAnn, listen..." the woman ordered as she grabbed hold of the man's hand. The teenager's eyes darted every- where, then rested on the ground.

"I'm not speaking to you, Tracy. I'm speaking to the father of the bride, who was meant to arrive yesterday."

"I can explain."

"Go on, then," LuAnn challenged him.

"Dad? Is that you?" Yasmine emerged from her cabana draped in a towel.

"Hello, darling."

"Don't *darling* me. Where were you? This isn't some turn-up-when-you-feel-like-it social club, it's your daughter's wedding, Max!"

Maximilian Cunningham glanced around at the people within earshot and gave a nervous laugh. "Now, now, sweetheart, that temper is very unbecoming. I came as soon as I could. All of this... this... build up is nice, but what matters is that I'm here in good time to walk Hattie down the aisle."

Hattie crossed her arms and huffed. "The vacancy's been filled, sorry."

"Hattie, dear, I can..." Cornelius began, but Hattie came to him and draped her arms around him.

"Daddy, meet Cornelius. He'll be giving me away tomorrow. So you might as well turn around and disappear back under the stone you just crawled out from."

Maximilian blinked, his mouth agape. His new wife pulled on his arm. The teenage boy continued to stare at a random spot on the ground as if it was reading him his fortune.

"We'll let you all calm down for a while and see you at dinner," the new wife, Tracy, simpered. She didn't quite make eye contact with any of the Cunninghams, who glared at her as if they were one perfectly trained and orchestrated army and she was the enemy.

Tracy led Maximilian away and when the teenager realised they were moving, he glanced across at the rest of us, gave an apologetic smile and a wave, and followed their retreat.

"Who the hell does he think he is just appearing from nowhere?" Yasmine exclaimed.

"He's got a cheek," Hattie agreed.

"He's not going to take kindly to anyone else giving you away, you know," Damson said.

One of the staff members approached LuAnn and whispered in her ear, and she flashed a smile. "We've lost enough time focusing on him and it's eating into our massage slot. Let's not keep these people waiting any longer."

Everyone followed her command without hesitation, and the masseuses who had emerged from cabanas discreetly returned inside.

No sooner had I followed my masseuse to a cabana and had the curtain pulled back so I could enter than there was a high-pitched scream nearby. I glanced at the masseuse for clues but she looked as alarmed as I felt.

Warily, we emerged from the cabana, our actions imitating those of everyone else. Peeking her head out of the cabana next to mine was Yasmine, her face flushed with annoyance.

"Is this some kind of prank? Because heaven help anyone who comes between me and this massage!" She moaned.

A petite woman in the hotel's uniform waved her hand in the air to get our attention. Her face was pale and even from a distance away I could see that her hand was shaking.

"What is it?" LuAnn called.

"Please fetch the manager. I'll stay here," the woman said, her tone as shaky as her hand.

"I'll go," another masseuse volunteered and dashed off out of sight.

As we waited, we slipped into an awkward silence and I used the time to look at everyone in the safety of knowing they were all too stunned to notice. We were a party member down, that was clear. Derrick Riches was nowhere in sight. And yet he'd been the first to get into his cabana, keen to get some new hands on his skin.

I shuddered at the thought. Perhaps he'd crossed a line with his masseuse and she was bringing the manager down here to tell him off. Maybe even to kick him off the grounds! That would surely make things easier for Yasmine.

The masseuse returned, a small suited man lagging behind her, his forehead damp with sweat.

"Ana, what's the issue? The Cunninghams are very special guests, we don't want to disrupt their day," he asked in between laboured breaths as he reached the cabanas.

Instead of answering, Ana simply pulled open the cabana curtain that she had been guarding. The manager glanced inside, leaned over, and promptly projectile vomited over his shiny brown loafers.

"What the heck is this?" LuAnn demanded and stormed across to the cabana. Ana attempted to pull the curtain back, but LuAnn was too quick for her.

She glanced inside, rolled her eyes and gave a short laugh. "Finally, someone's done him in!"

"The cameras are still rolling," Skye called out from the back of the crowd. Indeed, the camera crew were catching every scene of whatever calamity had happened. Was this all part of the plan? I'd heard that some of these reality TV shows were at least partly scripted.

"What's happened, mama?" Yasmine asked.

LuAnn closed her eyes, massaged the bridge of her nose, and let out a breath. "Our friend Derrick appears to have met an untimely end."

"He's dead?" Yasmine asked.

"He's more than dead judging by the size of the hole in the back of his head. He's been clobbered to death with your Reality TV Icon award, Yas! He's been murdered."

7

LuAnn's announcement stunned everyone into silence, apart from Yasmine who was distressed at the thought of her prized award being covered in blood.

"You brought it to my wedding?" Hattie asked in disbelief.

"I never leave it home unattended!" Yasmine said between heavy breaths.

It was Ana the masseuse who guided us all indoors, to a large and opulent ballroom that was set out ready for a wedding.

"You're kidding me? Rafe wasn't supposed to see any of this! Were there no other rooms you could take us to?"

"Hattie, that's enough," LuAnn ordered, and her daughter hushed.

Rafe took a seat next to his fiance and took her hand in his. "It's beautiful. You've done an incredible job. Are they real doves?"

I followed his gaze to the far corner, where a black cloth partially covered a gilded birdcage.

Hattie grinned. "Of course they are! Do you remember? You used to call me..."

"My little dove," Rafe glanced at the camera as he enunciated the words and planted a kiss on Hattie's forehead.

I caught Ana's gaze as she rolled her eyes.

The grand double doors opened and the manager emerged, his eyes bloodshot and his shoes foul smelling. Any semblance of authority he could have had was long gone, but we all looked to him for guidance still.

"I have called the police. Until they arrive, please stay here and don't discuss anything," he said, and with that he was gone. A click followed and Rafe jumped up out of his seat and sprinted to the door, which he tried in vain.

"He's locked us in! Doesn't he realise who we are! Doesn't he realise the plans Hattie has made?"

"It's okay, my love," Hattie said, but she beamed at him with love.

"We'll all need to speak to the police. It's best we do as he said," I explained.

"You get involved with a lot of murders?" Skye gave me a wink as he sprawled across three seats.

"Not if I can help it," I said. It was way too soon to share my minimal experience of solving murder mysteries.

"Emily here is an amateur sleuth! The best there is!" Cornelius exclaimed.

"Stop! He's joking," I laughed, while I shot Cornelius dead-eyes. The difficulty, of course, was that he didn't speak body language and was ignorant to all subtleties.

"Please, everyone quiet," Ana the masseuse commanded.

"Yes, let's all do as Ana says," LuAnn said, and the room fell silent, following LuAnn's word, nobody else's.

By the time the click was heard again and the door

opened, everyone was grouchy and starving. My stomach was doing flips to attract my attention.

Every table in the room had a fishbowl filled with retro candy, but Hattie refused to allow any to be eaten. That whole conversation had happened without a single word. Damson reached her hand into the fishbowl closest to her and Hattie had given her such a withering look, she'd pretended she had been just wanting to rub a smear off the inside of the glass.

The manager walked into the room, flanked on either side by a tall, slim police officer.

"We'll take it from here," they said in unison, and the manager gave a nod and departed. No click. At least we were no longer locked in.

8

"I'm officer Pedaro, this is my colleague, Jiminez. You're all witnesses to a serious crime, a murder of one Derrick Riches. We'll be separating you and questioning you one by one."

Hattie raised her arm.

"Yes?" Pedaro asked.

"Hi, erm, pleased to meet you. I'm Hattie. Hattie Cunningham, from *Keeping up with the Cunninghams...* you may know it?"

Pedaro stared at her blankly.

"Ha, no, well you're probably too busy fighting crime to watch TV, I guess."

"Not at all. I enjoy Dynasty very much," Pedaro deadpanned. "You have a question?"

"Yes, I..."

"Jiminez will answer that now for you."

"Of course. I can help you. Here's the answer: we are the ones asking the questions," Jiminez said with a sneer.

The officers laughed, and even Skye gave a chortle.

"Mama!" Hattie exclaimed.

LuAnn shook her head. "Do as you're told, Hat."

"You have a wise mother. Now, as I was saying, we are here to question you all one at a time. It's going to take some time, if my instincts are right. I suspect most of you are guilty of a serious crime."

"What? You haven't even spoken to us!" Yasmine exclaimed.

"You were right, boss," Jiminez muttered.

"I always am. Yes, you're all guilty of the serious crime of too much talking. That makes our job harder. We'll try to rein you in but some of you are going to talk and talk and talk and... you get the idea. It's very tiresome."

I glanced sidelong at Cornelius, whose face was one of pure innocence.

"We'll start with..."

The door opened, and in stormed Maximilian and the same entourage as earlier. A few seconds later, the manager ran in, still green-faced and smelly.

"I'm sorry, I tried to stop them," the manager panted.

Pedaro cast the man away with a wave of his hand and looked at the three new arrivals. "Who are you?"

"I'm the father of the bride, that's who I am. Who the hell are you? I was down at reception complaining about the thread count of my bedding when I hear that man with the disgusting shoes talking about locking my family up in here! You'd better have some answers, boyo!" Maximilian demanded.

Pedaro and Jiminez moved in unison again and held out their police badges.

"Police. I see. Well, okay then. What's happened? Are my girls at risk?"

Yasmine rolled her eyes. "What if we are? Are you our knight in shining armour, daddy?"

"Are we in danger?" Hattie asked as she climbed into Rafe's lap and snuggled into him.

"Nobody is in danger. Anymore. You three must leave," Pedaro said.

"Actually, they were by the cabanas as well. If you're speaking to all of us, you should speak to them too," I said.

Yasmine side-eyed me, her eyes narrowed.

"Just what we need. More people who love to talk. Fine. Names?"

"Maximilian   Anders   Cartwright   McQueen Cunningham."

"Seriously?" Pedaro asked.

Maximilian nodded. "It's a fine name. I was named after my..."

"Alright, that's enough. You?"

"Tracy Cunningham."

"Becker   Cunningham-Brown,"   the   teenage   boy murmured.

"Take a seat. You're going to be here some time. Jiminez, go out and ask for some food and drink."

Jiminez nodded and left the room.

Pedaro eyed us and finally fixed his gaze on LuAnn. "I admit, I've seen a few episodes, and you're one impressive lady. I don't know why he left you. It never made sense to me. What were you thinking, Maximilian Anders Cartwright McQueen Cunningham?"

Maximilian pursed his lips. "You can call me Mr Cunningham, and my personal life is none of your business. I don't even know who's died."

"You shouldn't know that anyone's died yet, Maxie. Let me make sure I record that little goof in my notebook. Here we go: *suspect reveals knowing more than they should*. Great start to the case. Wait 'til I tell Jiminez."

Maximilian pinched the bridge of his nose. "You've got all of your suspects locked in a room, it's pretty obvious what's going on here. This tactic's straight out of an Agatha Christie novel!"

Pedaro looked him up and down and smiled. "You don't look like a Christie fan. How sweet. For the record, it was hotel staff who locked the door, not me. But thanks for your recommendation that we treat everyone here as suspects, not witnesses. It's always handy to have information from someone who knows the personalities involved. Although, not an issue here, since everyone who watches TV knows *these* personalities."

So he did know the programme! And didn't sound like a fan.

The door opened again and Jiminez slipped in.

"They're bringing in some sandwiches," he told Pedaro.

"Sandwiches? We were expecting smoothies," LuAnn exclaimed.

"Yeah, I don't eat gluten," Damson said.

"I don't eat carbs! Especially not this close to my wedding!" Hattie wailed.

"To eat the sandwiches or not to eat the sandwiches, that is the question. I'll leave you with that important question while I do my own important questioning. You? Let's go," Pedaro grunted as he cocked his finger like a gun in LuAnn's direction.

She straightened her back and followed him out of the grand room, leaving Jiminez to stand guard.

"He's a funny guy. Very funny guy. But he can crack a case. Don't you worry about that."

"Really, Derrick's murderer going unpunished isn't an idea that will keep me up at night," Yasmine said.

Jiminez hushed her, and the room fell into an awkward silence.

The sandwiches were wheeled in on a silver trolley and sat, curling in the heat. Nobody wanted to be the first to admit to be thinking of their stomach at such a time.

The restraint would be causing Cornelius physical pain, I was sure, but when I glanced a peek at him, he was fast asleep, his head tipped back and his mouth wide open.

LuAnn was escorted back to the room and looked visibly shaken by the ordeal. Pedaro selected Yasmine and led her out.

"Are you okay?" Maximilian asked his ex-wife as Tracy glared at him.

"That man... he took me into a broom cupboard!" LuAnn exclaimed.

Maximilian reared up, horrified, and approached Jiminez. "What is this? How dare you treat my family this way? We're not under arrest, are we?"

"Well, no... not yet," Jiminez said with a laugh.

"That's it. We're not going to stand for this. Please, the rest of you go. I'll wait here for Yasmine," Maximilian said.

"If I may?" I rose to my feet, my voice timid. "We're not under arrest because we're witnesses. This is perfectly normal procedure. The police want to speak to us. We should help them."

"And who are you? Are you a cop, too?"

"No!" I said with a nervous laugh.

"I need to find some real food. I'm out of here," Damson said.

"Me too," Becker agreed.

One by one, the group reduced until only Maximilian and I remained in the room with Jiminez. Cornelius was present, too, but his snoring confirmed he hadn't made an active choice to stay.

Tracy had left only following a drawn out hug and a deep kiss, as if this was war times and one of them was about to go off into active duty.

"Pedaro won't be happy about this," Jiminez chuckled, and I felt a nervous roll in my gut for the rest of them. Walking out on a police investigation? Sure, it was possible. It was within their rights. But it was so far out of my comfort zone I could barely fathom it out.

I wished Cornelius was awake so he could guide me. Did we look guilty by staying? Did the others look guilty by leaving?

Derrick Riches was dead! Yasmine Cunningham's first husband. The man who had discovered her. It would be a huge news story when it broke, and news of that size never took long to break. It was plausible that someone at the hotel had already contacted a journalist and sold the exclusive story for a life-changing sum of money.

I considered the reaction to his death. Nobody in the wedding party had seemed overly upset. Yasmine had her reasons for disliking him. In fact, the whole family probably did, even though there was an argument that all of their wealth and success was only because of his initial involvement.

The dislike for him wasn't a surprise. But if it was so universal, who had cared enough to invite him out here? And why?

As I got deeper into the rabbit hole of my mind, the door opened and Yasmine appeared, Pedaro behind her.

"Where is everyone? Where's mama?"

"I told them to leave. And now you and I will also leave," Maximilian strode across the room and took his daughter's hand in his. To my surprise, Pedaro didn't block the way and in fact held the door open for them, but Yasmine turned back and looked at me.

"Are you coming?"

"I'm going to speak to the officers. I'll catch up with you after?"

She nodded, and then her father yanked on her arm, and she was gone.

Pedaro closed the door and raised an eyebrow at Jiminez, who shrugged.

"Who won?" Pedaro asked.

Jiminez consulted the heavy gold watch draped on his wrist. "They left twenty-three minutes in."

"Damn it!" Pedaro reached into his pocket, pulled out a wallet, and handed a few notes to Jiminez.

"What are you doing?" I asked.

"Oh, just a little side hustle we enjoy. How long until the Americans storm off and refuse to talk without their lawyers present! Jiminez is unbeatable. I was pretty sure the Cunninghams would break within five minutes."

"I want my lawyer!" Jiminez cried in a mock-American accent, and they both burst into laughter.

"That was good!"

"You cheated though, boss. You were even more irritating than you are normally, trying to get them to stop talking."

"That wasn't even for the bet. You know I've got that dinner with Kim tonight. If I missed it, she'd cut off my pinkie finger and feed me that."

Jiminez let out a low whistle. "I gotta get me a woman like that."

"Hold on," I found my voice. "Do you not even want to speak to us?"

"What I want, sweetheart, is to be over at Rosita's drinking a cold one. She stores the pint glasses in the freezer, can you believe that? I drink enough of those, I come away with chilblains. That's what I want to be doing! What I have to be doing for exactly three more hours today is keeping the good streets of this city safe and clean. If that means speaking to a bunch of privileged tourists moan about eating sandwiches for lunch, that's what I have to do."

"Well I'm not privileged, and I'm not moaning about anything apart from the fact that a man has been killed and the officers investigating don't seem that motivated. So how about you take my statement?"

The officers blinked at each other, but they weren't as shocked as I was by my outburst. I decided to reach for a sandwich, just to prove that I wasn't ungrateful for them, and regretted it as soon as my fingers made contact with the hardened bread. Mexican weather was on a whole other level.

Pedaro crossed his arms and gave me a withering look, then tilted his head to indicate that I should follow him. He led me out of the grand room and across the hallway into a small office that did, indeed, hold a broom in the corner. The office was actually quite nice and much tidier than the one Cornelius had at home.

Pedaro took a seat behind the desk and gestured for me to sit across from him.

"Quite the outspoken one, huh?"

I couldn't help but laugh. "I'm actually the exact opposite."

"Well now's not the time to go quiet on me. I presume you know something? You have some solid intel for me?"

My mouth dropped open. "Oh, no, no. I don't know anything."

"Come on, lady. Horrible ex husband bashed in by his scorned wife's hideous statue? It's hardly the mystery of the century!"

"You think Yasmine clubbed him to death with her own award? Isn't that a bit obvious?"

Pedaro shrugged. "You tell me. You know these people."

"I've never even met Derrick Riches before today."

"You're Yasmine Cunningham's best friend and you never met her first husband?"

"What? I..."

Pedaro closed his eyes and tilted his head skyward. He was either praying for me to be a better witness, or thinking of his evening plans with Kim.

"Let's not lie about the innocent things, okay? That's such a sloppy way to get caught. If you killed Mr Riches, I want you to either confess right now or never get caught. Or maybe let me figure it out using my inferior brain power, right? Please don't make yourself suspicious because you lie about innocent things."

"I think you mean superior, not inferior," I mumbled.

"Just testing. Now, I've spoken to Yasmine Cunningham, she's explained everything. She told me who was here. You're the best friend. It's not for me to question why a super glamorous celebrity like her has a fairly plain and ordinary best friend like you. I don't understand female friendship. Maybe you used to be best friends but you've made another friend and promised to be their best friend, so you don't feel you can sit here and not tell me about that other friend... but you can believe me when I say I don't care. For my purposes, you are the best friend, yes?"

"Yes," I agreed, too stunned to argue. Yasmine had described me as her best friend? We only met the day before. Maybe she thought it would be too confusing to explain the truth.

"Somehow, you hadn't met Mr Riches until today. From what I hear, you can manage not to be too sad about that. Yasmine hated him, right?"

I weighed up the question. Yes, she did seem to hate him. But he was an ex. Most people seemed to hate their exes. Not that I had any personal experience in that situation.

"Things ended badly between them," I said.

"And yet here he was. Attending her sister's wedding. What was all that about?"

"I don't know," I admitted.

"You don't know much for a woman so determined to stick around and take up my time," Pedaro grumbled.

"All I can tell you is that Yasmine seemed as surprised as anyone when he arrived. He's not the only one, either. You know her other ex-husband, Wayne Jones?"

"Never heard of him."

"He was her second husband. He's here too."

"He wasn't in the list we were given by the hotel," Pedaro said.

"He didn't join us for the massages. He went to the bar."

"So, he's not a witness. You scared me then, made me think I had another person to get through! Thank the Lord for this Wayne Jones and his good sense to skip a massage!" Pedaro kissed his fingertips and raised them upwards.

"I don't get it. Don't you want to solve this case?"

Pedaro clutched his chest and took on a look of having been offended. "What are you suggesting? Are you implying that this rich American idiot who had the dumb luck to get killed by a reality TV award isn't top of my priorities? I'm wounded. Really."

"Okay. I get it. But I'm telling you everything I can because it's the right thing to do. You can speak to my uncle, too, and then you should be able to get home for your dinner."

"What does your uncle know?"

"You'd have to ask him!" I snapped.

Pedaro shrugged. "Your uncle's the one in there asleep? Looks a bit like a walrus?"

"That's him."

"He saw nothing. I won't waste his time with a statement."

"How can you be so sure? You haven't asked him a single question."

"Emily, you're okay but you're naive. Let me tell you, it takes decades to get this cynical, and even I couldn't help but learn a thing or two in that time. Generally speaking, people don't go to sleep right after witnessing a murder. Or after committing a murder," Pedaro said with a wink.

"You don't know Uncle C," I mumbled, but Pedaro was already up off his feet. He held open the office door and I got up from the chair and followed him.

By the time we returned, Uncle C was awake and confused.

"Did I miss the wedding?"

"No," I said with a laugh.

"Ah, good. I have a habit of that. Did I ever tell you about Rita Malone's second wedding? I snored my way through the whole thing, which got me in some bother as she was still harbouring those feelings for me. She thought I was pretending to be asleep to cause a scene! But I was dead to the world. I can't be blamed really, the speeches droned on and on and on. Some people really can talk, lassie!"

Jiminez raised his eyebrows.

"Okay, well thanks for everything. We'll be in touch," Pedaro clapped his hands.

"You don't want to speak to me?"

"No, no thank you, sir. Your niece here has been very helpful. We'll be in touch if we need anything further," Pedaro said in a panic.

"Ah, that's grand. Well done, Em. Did she tell you how she came into my life? It's a fascinating story if you've got a minute."

Jiminez's radio crackled and the two officers looked at each other as if the interruption was heaven sent.

"Another time, sir. We need to get going," Pedaro said with a grin.

"Of course, of course," Cornelius took the rejection well and we left the room and returned to the hotel foyer in a state of disbelief.

"I can't believe there's been a murder. How do we keep getting caught up in these things?" I whispered.

Cornelius grinned at me, his eyes half-hidden beneath his bushy eyebrows. "Isn't it fun, lassie? Have you got any suspects in mind yet?"

"What? No! The police are dealing with it," I protested.

"And you have faith in them? Persuaded by our friend Pedaro, were you? What kind of a murder investigator doesn't grill every single witness when he has the chance? We could leave the country tomorrow for all he knows!"

"That's true. He didn't ask me how long we'd be here for," I admitted.

"Exactly. So, let's share our ideas over a nice cup of tea!" Cornelius suggested as he pressed the call button for the lift.

Safely back in the Opal Suite with a mug of tea each, we sat out on the balcony and gazed out at the water. It was a beautiful day and I was in paradise, but a man had been killed. The juxtaposition was sobering.

"Do you want to go first?" I asked.

"If you're sure, lassie. You know I don't like to take over a conversation. But I had a little snooze back there and it's helped the little grey cells. The way I see it, we have to figure out who benefits from Derrick being dead. Who wanted him dead?"

"It seems like all of them! He was an unpopular man, nobody liked him," I admitted.

"And yet he was invited here."

"So somebody must like him?"

"Or whoever invited him here is the killer," Cornelius said.

"And they invited him here so they could kill him!" I exclaimed. I was grateful we were so high up. This was not a conversation for the people down by the pool to overhear. Murder and margaritas were not the best mix.

"It's a possibility, right? Do we actually know who invited him and Wayne?"

"Nobody's admitted it to me," I said. The whisper of an idea began to form in my mind but it was too early for me to reach out and grasp it.

"I discussed it with LuAnn and she seemed surprised to see them both," Cornelius said.

"What was her opinion of Derrick?"

"She's a sophisticated lady is LuAnn. Did you know that she can do the splits? I mean, I haven't seen her do it yet but can you imagine? The woman has endless talents," Cornelius adopted a dreamy voice and gazed into the distance.

"But what did she say about Derrick?" I prompted.

"Ah, yes. I was just getting to that. She didn't say much, but it's clear she's not a fan of his."

"Well, I understand that things didn't end well between him and Yasmine. LuAnn's a protective mum. She wouldn't be happy with him after that."

"Great idea! Let's read up on why the marriage failed," Cornelius grabbed his phone and tap-tapped away on it.

"Whatever the media says might not be the truth," I said.

"True, true. Here we go! *Yasmine Cunningham divorce final. Cunningham, star of Keeping up with the Cunninghams, is officially a single lady again after her divorce from Derrick Riches was finalised this week. Cunningham began divorce proceedings after...* hold on... goodness... what a..."

"What? What is it?" I leaned in and tried to read his screen. He held it across to me.

"*Cunningham began divorce proceedings after discovering that Riches had been siphoning her money to fund a gambling addiction. Cunningham also made allegations that Riches had been pressuring her to appear in adult movies produced by his company, WAY2RICHES. Riches denied any wrongdoing but agreed to a divorce settlement that included him paying her over $27 million.*"

"He should have been killed just for naming his company that. What a buffoon," Cornelius muttered.

"If he paid Yasmine $27 million, do you think that was a repayment of the money he'd stolen from her?"

"I'd take a fairly safe bet on it, lassie. I don't like this one bit, I'll admit."

"Yasmine had a strong motive to want him dead, but surely she'd moved on with her life. If she was going to hurt him, wouldn't she have done that back then? Why wait until her sister's wedding?"

"You're right. Unless something happened since he arrived here. We don't know who invited Derrick, but we also don't know why he accepted the invitation. Would you, if you were him?"

"No way! I'd be too embarrassed to ever want to see the Cunninghams again," I said.

"Derrick seemed to me like a man who always had a plan. If he was here, there's every chance he was up to no good."

I sighed. "And we have absolutely no idea what that plan might have been."

Cornelius leaned over and squeezed my shoulder. "You're not going to give up at the first hurdle, are you Em? That's not the niece I know and..."

"Know and what? Were you going to say love, Uncle C?" I asked with a grin.

His cheeks flushed a furious red, angry as a beet, and he jumped up from his chair. "I'm going to go and rest my eyes for a bit. All of this sun and excitement is taking it out of me."

"It's time for the beach walk in a few minutes," I reminded him.

He shrugged a wide shoulder. "Nobody will go for the beach walk now. Not after a man has been killed. It's insensitive."

"Okay. I'll wake you for dinner?" I called, but he was already out of earshot, and it was mere seconds later that the suite began to almost shake with the vibrations of his snoring.

All alone, my mind returned to the sight of Derrick, sprawled out on the massage bed, all soft towel and no dignity. The man seemed from all evidence to be an absolute wretch, and yet I felt that familiar itch inside me begin to grow. I couldn't stand by and ignore the puzzle of who killed him, not to mention how and why.

I washed our tea mugs, put them to dry, put them away, then paced the suite until I realised my restlessness would only be solved by me taking action.

I quickly scrawled a note for Cornelius advising him that I was going to walk the beach alone, then slipped back into my flip flops and left the suite.

9

The air conditioning in the hallways was so powerful I was almost tempted to go back and grab a cardigan, but I knew the sun was out and the balcony had been incredibly warm, so I called for the lift and made my way out to the designated meeting point for the private beach walk.

To my surprise, the Cunninghams were all gathered by the meeting point, sipping a pre-walk glass of champagne. The mood seemed muted and everyone was quiet.

Yasmine saw me and waved, and I went to her side, like the loyal best friend that Pedaro believed me to be.

"How are you holding up?" I asked.

"Oh, I'm fine. I feel awful, of course."

"That's natural."

"I know. I just can't stop thinking about it... I feel so terrible."

"You mustn't blame yourself," I soothed.

"It's my fault he was here! I'm the one who got us all mixed up with Derrick. And now I just can't stop thinking about poor Hattie."

"Poor Hattie?" I realised we had been talking at cross purposes. I'd imagined she was feeling bad for Derrick, but apparently not.

"Derrick's going to get all of the season finale interest now, isn't he? He'll be down there laughing."

I took down there to mean Hell, and wasn't too sure anyone down there laughed much apart from the guy with the red tail.

"That's why we all have to stick with the plan, Emily. We've got to throw ourselves into these activities like our lives depend on it."

"Maybe they do. Maybe poor old Derrick was killed because he was being a wedding bore," Skye said with a wink as he stood beside me and draped a lazy arm around Yasmine.

"Good afternoon, all! Please follow me, I will be your guide for this wonderful walk. My name is Roberto, and I am delighted to share with you our completely private and stunningly beautiful beach. Now, look to the end of the beach, I would suggest you go as far as the white hut you see down there, my colleagues will have champagne ready, you can sit and enjoy the sunset and then begin the walk back to me."

"You won't be coming with us?" LuAnn asked. She had dressed in a leopard print flowing kaftan and looked every inch the goddess my uncle had decided she was.

"Ah, no. For this walk, I understand the bride and groom prefer privacy with loved ones," Roberto explained.

The group of us stood on the boardwalk, warm sand seeping between our toes. The beach was golden, the sea was clear, and the sun was beginning its evening descent.

"Is that wise, Hat?" LuAnn called.

Hattie and Rafe were already walking across the sand,

hand in hand, and LuAnn's question wasn't answered. Hattie was dressed in a long white gown that looked almost bridal, while Rafe was topless, his back glistening with sweat as they leisurely strolled across the beach.

The scene was such a photo opportunity, I could barely believe the camera crew weren't present. No sooner had I had that thought than the flash of a camera erupted.

Damson rolled her eyes, grabbed what looked like an ethics textbook, and stormed back to the hotel. Becker followed her.

Maximilian and Tracy were nowhere in sight, and I wondered whether the itinerary had been hidden from them deliberately.

Yasmine narrowed her eyes and followed the direction of the flash, but whoever had taken the picture was hiding from view.

"Can you believe this? I swear, the paparazzi have me bugged or something. How did they find us? " Yasmine exclaimed.

"Yes, I can believe it. Well, let's give them something worth their trouble," LuAnn said with a smile, and she stepped onto the sand and confidently walked after Hattie and Rafe.

"Go on, Yasmine. You're not camera shy."

"Wow. Really, Wayne?"

He had the decency to blush. "Sorry. That was uncalled for."

"You know, we've already had one person not survive this trip, man," Skye said as he sidled closer to Yasmine and shot Wayne a look of the cat that's got the cream.

"Hold on, what does that mean? Are you threatening me?" Wayne asked.

"Of course he isn't. Skye, go and check on my mum. Please?" Yasmine pleaded.

"Seriously?"

"Yes, seriously. I'll be fine with Emily."

Skye rolled his eyes, but trudged along the sand and linked his arm through LuAnn's, who startled at his touch. She seemed awfully jumpy. Derrick's murder must have really got to her.

There was another explosion of light as a camera flashed, and Yasmine turned and glared in the direction the paparazzi must be.

"We'll never return to this hotel, Roberto. You assured me this would be private!"

"It is, it is! I don't understand. They must be on the Hibiscus Suite Balcony. If you remember, your party also booked that suite in order to ensure this privacy. It's impossible that anyone could be there. The only key was given to your family at check in!"

Yasmine's mouth was set in a stern line. "Well, clearly there's a second key. Or you've got a case of breaking and entering."

"Or someone gave the paparazzi the key," I croaked.

"What?" Yasmine turned to me, her eyes narrowed.

"It's possible, Yas. I mean, Hattie didn't seem too upset by the cameras flashing," Wayne said.

"Neither did my mother!"

"See? It's a possibility at least," I said.

"And what does it even matter? The whole thing's going to be shown on TV. Any privacy argument here is pretty ridiculous."

"It's not about privacy. It's about exclusivity. You wouldn't understand, Wayne."

"Oh, I understand, all right. Your family see everything in terms of the headlines it can create, the pay day it can be. Why do you all want more when you have too much already?"

Yasmine swallowed and her eyes filled. At that moment, a camera flashed and almost blinded me.

"They can see us," I groaned. I had no desire to see my own face on the front page of a glossy magazine. Hopefully they'd be able to crop me out of the scene, and focus on Yasmine. Not that I wanted the paparazzi to hound her, although she did seem better able to deal with them than I was.

"Let's walk," Wayne commanded, and I watched as he reached for Yasmine's hand. To my surprise, she let him, and the three of us headed out across the sand. LuAnn and Skye were not far ahead, dawdling as LuAnn stopped to examine shells. Hattie and Rafe had gone down to the water's edge and were standing, hand in hand, gazing out at the sea.

"I'm glad you came," Yasmine murmured as we walked.

Wayne shrugged, his muscular shoulders clearly visible through the thin cotton shirt. "I didn't want to see you, but I couldn't say no."

"I am sorry about what happened. You know that, don't you?"

"How would I know that? You're still making the same mistakes now, Yas. Skye isn't the guy for you. He'll have broken your heart within a year."

"Oh, I know. The public love us as a couple, though. That's true, isn't it Emily?"

I gave a nervous laugh. I wasn't sure that I was qualified to comment on what the public loved, but I suspected she was right. Skye Portillo was the man of the moment. It made sense for him to fall madly in love with Yasmine Cunningham, the It Girl. It was like the ultimate version of the prom king and queen being the most popular people in school. Not that any school I'd ever been to had had a prom, never mind a king or queen. England didn't buy into all of that stuff. Maybe having genuine royalty made it that way.

"I guess it makes a good story," I said.

Wayne groaned. "But Yas, this is your life. Who cares whether it makes a good story? Do you even love him?"

Yasmine glanced at me, then back at Wayne. "I don't think that's any of your business."

"Look, I'm going to go on ahead. I'll catch you later," I may not have been any kind of love expert, but I knew the conversation was not meant for my ears.

I quickened my pace and easily caught up with LuAnn. Skye was no longer walking beside her, and was instead heading straight to the white champagne hut, his head down, hands in his pockets. Had he seen Yasmine and Wayne and flew into a jealous rage? Or was he just really desperate for a glass of Moet?

"Hey," I said as I approached LuAnn. I didn't want to just reach her side and alarm her.

"Oh, honey! Hello! Where's that dashing father of yours?" LuAnn asked with a grin. It seemed too late to explain that Cornelius was not my father, and I certainly didn't want to get into the fact that my actual father hadn't even returned my last few calls. It was easier to just play along.

"He needed a nap. I'm sure he'll join us later," I said.

"He'd better! I can't wait to hear him at the karaoke," she said with a laugh.

"Oh, trust me, you might regret making that wish," I said, and we both giggled, then descended into a comfortable silence.

"Are you okay? You seem a bit jumpy," I asked.

"Oh, I'm okay honey. It's such a shame that the occasion's been tarnished with that awful man."

"Derrick?"

LuAnn nodded and her dangling pearl earrings danced. "I'd like to know who invited him. I really would."

"So it wasn't you?"

"Of course not! He was bad enough first time around, why on earth would I want him back here with my family? Near my Yasmine? He was bad news, Emily. I knew it as soon as I saw him."

"He played a big role in Yasmine's career, didn't he?"

"He was taking a cut of everything! The best thing I did was get her out of that deal and start managing her myself. Derrick wanted her to go down such a dark path... adult movies and all kinds of things that might seem fun when you're that young and desperate for fame, but then you get older and they stay with you."

"Was she desperate for fame?" I asked.

LuAnn laughed. "Oh, only from the moment she could walk. She had the lead role in every school play, the solo in every concert, she was the face of the high school newspaper every week. And between me and you, she's a beautiful girl but she never could act or sing. She was born for the attention. It was only a matter of time before she was discovered."

"And she still likes the attention now?"

"I think so. She can moan about the paparazzi at times, but if they stopped following her, she wouldn't know what to do with herself."

"That's interesting," I said.

"How so?"

"Erm... I don't know. I guess it's hard for me to imagine your lives. I'd hate the pressure of it all."

LuAnn frowned. "It's not like that for the rest of us. Sure, we have the show, but we all know that this life is because of Yasmine. If she decides to call it a day, we'll be yesterday's news."

"Oh," I was unsure what else to say.

"That's why we have to live for today only," she said, then grinned. "And I really am looking forward to seeing Cornelius later."

We headed out towards the water, where Hattie and Rafe were locked in a tight embrace, their arms grasped around each other.

As we got closer, it was clear that Hattie was in tears, and we caught the end of a sentence, her tone sharp and pained. Before we could retreat, she noticed us, looked up, flashed us a bright smile.

"Sorry, you caught me having a moment. Isn't this the most beautiful day?"

Rafe kissed the top of her head and extracted himself from her clutch. "The emotions are getting the better of Hattie today, I'm afraid."

"Well, she's entitled to be something of a drama queen on the eve of her wedding. Rafe, be a darling and give us a minute?"

Rafe bristled at the suggestion.

"I can go as well," I volunteered.

"No, dear, you stay. Sometimes a lady needs female support. You know, Rafe, there are women's issues to discuss," LuAnn pressed.

Rafe's cheeks flamed at the mention of women's issues, just as I knew Uncle C's would if he were here. He gave a brisk nod and headed off across the sand, where I could make out the shape of several people sprawled on white Adirondack chairs outside the Champagne Hut.

I squinted and saw that Cornelius was among them, identifiable by his rotund shape and spectacular beard. He appeared to be wearing a sombrero.

I glanced behind and saw that Yasmine was approaching us, alone. Wayne was no longer with her. Had Skye seen the two of them together? My stomach flipped with nervous tension.

"Right, Hat, what's going on? Is it just emotions?" LuAnn asked, her voice more stern than I'd anticipate.

Hattie took a shaky breath and nodded. "Everything's fine, mama."

"A lot of people are relying on things going ahead tomorrow without a hitch," LuAnn said.

"No hitches apart from you getting hitched!" Yasmine joked.

"Yasmine, please."

"Sorry."

"Hat, if there's an issue, you have to tell us now. Well, no, you should have told us weeks ago. Now, the emotions are understandable, this is a beautiful day and it's all so overwhelming. Champagne will help. Come along," LuAnn reached for Hattie's hand and we all began a slow and leisurely stroll across to the champagne hut.

"Oh, daddy's there," Hattie exclaimed and I saw that Maximilian was indeed sat next to Cornelius.

"Better late than never," LuAnn said under her breath. "Oh, Lord help us. What is Tracy wearing? Is that Gucci from last season?"

To my inexperienced eyes, Tracy appeared to be wearing a simple white beach dress, but I saw LuAnn stand a little straighter as she took in the second wife's fashion faux pas.

"Mommy, don't be mean," Yasmine said. She seemed quiet, deflated in some way. I wondered what had happened during her walk with Wayne.

"Ah, here comes the bride! My beautiful daughter, what a sight you are!" Maximilian climbed out of the Adirondack and enveloped Hattie in a crushing hug. I thought I saw him even sniff her hair as he held her.

"Thank you, daddy," Hattie said as she pulled away slightly.

"Champagne?" Tracy offered. She held a glass out and Hattie accepted. The move seemed like a peace offering and I found myself oddly sentimental. Families came in all forms.

"Ah, lassie, come and help an old man out of a silly chair!" Cornelius called out, and everyone laughed. I gladly stepped away from the Cunningham bubble for a moment and grabbed one of his arms, but my pulls were in vain. I lacked the strength needed to move him.

"Here, I'll help," Wayne's voice came, and he grabbed both of Cornelius' hands in his own and pulled with all of his might. I thought for a moment that Wayne would end up flat on his back in the sand, but he managed to keep his balance as Uncle C rose, victorious, from the chair.

"Excellent, excellent! You, young man, are a hero and a gentleman! You know, this reminds me of the time I came up against a hairy scene involving quicksand and a rattlesnake. I'd tell you who helped me out then, but you wouldn't believe me!"

Wayne grinned. "Go on, give me a clue?"

Uncle C leaned in, lapping up the attention. It occurred to me that he was a man who would have enjoyed - and deserved - his own reality show. "Let's just say this little lady did more than just stand over air vents in white dresses."

"No! Marilyn Monroe?" Wayne was wide-eyed.

I tried not to look cynical, but I felt fairly sure that I'd have already heard about any encounters my uncle had had with the screen idol.

"I can say no more. DiMaggio would have a fit if he heard!"

Wayne laughed and clapped Cornelius on the shoulder. "Okay, your secret's safe with me, sir."

"Oh, look!" Hattie gushed, and we all followed her gaze as the sun lowered in the sky, as if it was going to be submerged in the sea's glistening depths. Hattie instinctively reached out and held the hands of her mum and dad. Tracy gave Maximilian a smile of permission, and he relaxed into his daughter's affection.

The scene was truly magical, its beauty interrupted only by the wait staff from the champagne hut, who busied themselves collecting empty glasses.

I mouthed a silent thank you to a young woman as she took my glass from my hand, and she nodded that I was welcome before retreating to the back of the hut, where I guessed the kitchen was, or perhaps even a beach buggy that would collect the supplies. The hut itself didn't appear large enough to store much of anything, or to house a sink.

No sooner had she disappeared than a high-pitched scream came from the direction in which she'd gone. The beautiful moment was interrupted.

Rafe was the first to respond. He dashed from the back of the group across the sand in an awkward attempt to run, and the rest of us followed.

There were two people lying on the sand behind the hut; the woman who had just taken my champagne glass, and Skye Portillo. While the woman appeared peaceful, blood seeped from a wound on Skye's chest. A bottle of expensive

champagne, smashed so the neck was spiked and dangerous, lay next to him, clotted with his blood.

"No!" Yasmine cried, just as Wayne pulled her close and
covered her eyes.

"Don't look. You hear me? Do not look, not even for a
second," he told her as her body spasmed in his arms, her
whole tiny form convulsing with sobs.

"Does anyone know First Aid?" Uncle C asked with a
nervous laugh.

"I do," came a young, unfamiliar voice. It was Becker. He
approached Skye first, checked for a pulse, then eyed his
mother and shook his head.

"How about the girl?"

Becker moved across to her, but as soon as he took her
hand in his, her eyes opened. She immediately sat up and
attempted to back away across the sand. The poor woman
was terrified.

"He's... he's dead, isn't he?" She stuttered.

"What happened here?" Maximilian asked her, his voice
booming and dripping with authority.

"You're asking me? I know nothing! I came with the
glasses and he was lying here," the woman sobbed.

"Okay, okay now. No need to cry. What's your name?"

"Sofia," she hiccuped.

"Alright, Sofia. Now just tell us what happened. Did he
get a bit too handsy with you? Is that it?" Maximilian
suggested.

"I wouldn't put it past him," LuAnn muttered.

"Handsy?"

"Did he try to touch you?" Maximilian clarified.

"What? No! You're not listening. He was like this already.
I came across, I saw him, I screamed, and I fainted," Sofia
cried, her tone desperate.

"She's telling the truth," I said.

"What makes you say that?"

"She collected my glass and I watched her walk over here. She screamed right away, and Rafe ran right over. There was no time for anything else to have happened," I looked to Rafe for confirmation.

"Oh, I don't know about that. I'm no athlete!" Rafe deflected.

"You weren't running the 800 metres, lad. It was a few feet. Even I could do that quickly and my days of being a threat to Roger Bannister are long gone," Cornelius said.

"I guess," Rafe said with a smile, as if the whole point of the conversation was his athletic prowess.

"Can we focus? This is clearly a murder. A second murder! We need to get help," I looked around, hoping a member of the hotel's staff would spring into action, but any staff based at the Champagne Hut appeared to have disappeared, apart from Sofia, who had got to her feet and was deliberately not looking down at Skye.

"I'll go and call the police," she volunteered.

"You're not going anywhere! We should make a citizen's arrest!" Rafe exclaimed.

"She isn't the killer," I said.

"Well, it's not one of us!" Maximilian shouted.

I said nothing further. One of the wedding party clearly was the killer, but that opinion obviously wasn't welcome. I couldn't blame Maximilian for wanting to cling to certainty, but the facts spoke for themselves.

"Who brought their mobile?" I asked.

The group stared at me, expressions blank.

"Your cell phones, lassie means. I've got mine, don't worry. Shall I call it in?" Cornelius asked.

I nodded to him.

The air was growing chilly as the sun disappeared, and I shivered.

Cornelius moved away and did the closest to a whisper that he could manage while we all tried to pretend we weren't listening. Yasmine remained in Wayne's arms, her face pressed against his chest.

"Right, I've left a message for that Pedaro guy. He's out apparently."

"What do we do in the meantime? We can't just leave him here," Yasmine asked, her voice muffled by Wayne's top.

"We need to stay together. Let's all move around to the front of the hut and wait until the police get here," I said.

"I'm not staying here. This drama's ruined enough of this trip and it's not taking a moment longer!" Hattie said. She crossed her arms and stuck out her bottom lip, like a child being sent to their bedroom too early.

Before anyone else could object, the heavens opened and a sudden, torrential down-pouring began. Everyone ducked under the narrow awning outside the Hut, and we watched in horror as the sky was illuminated by bolts of lightning.

"Inside, everyone! Now!" Maximilian commanded. He slipped into the authoritative mode like putting on an old glove.

Nobody argued with him.

10

I nside the Champagne Hut, the space was bigger than it appeared.

The Hut was made up of the main space which housed a fairly shabby bar, a sink piled with dirty glasses, and a scant flooring made up of wooden boardwalk planks. There was as much sand inside the Hut as outside it, but it had electricity, and it was dry.

I breathed a sigh of relief as I realised that the roof - which appeared to be straw - must have something more substantial supporting it. The heavens had truly opened, but not a drop made it inside.

"Now what do we do?" Hattie whined.

"I'll call the hotel and let them know we're here. They'll send someone out for us," Maximilian said with a shrug. He plucked his cell phone out of his pocket and dialled.

As he said hello, he pushed open the only internal door, and I caught a glimpse of a small stock room stacked high with bottles of champagne and various gins. There were a few empty crates, and piles of what looked to be discarded promotional material.

Maximilian's tone was stern, then agitated, then bewildered. He was a man used to getting his way, to having his every desire met without so much as a question, and it was clear that the call was not going to plan.

"And how about the dead man? Should I reassure him, too?" Maximilian snarled as he returned from the store cupboard, then ended the call.

"I see your people skills are still excellent, Max," LuAnn said with a smirk.

Tracy dashed to her husband's side, slender hands and long fingernails draped across him as she claimed her territory. Not that LuAnn looked the least bit interested in challenging her rights to ownership.

"What did they say, daddy?"

Maximilian pinched the bridge of his nose.

"What's wrong, hun?" Tracy asked, eyes wide with concern.

"I've got a migraine coming," he muttered.

"It'll be the change in weather. I did warn you that this climate might not be good for you," Tracy fussed.

"Really sorry about the headache and all, dad, but what did they say on the phone?" Yasmine asked, her arms folded.

"It's a migraine! Not a headache!" Tracy exclaimed.

I exchanged a glance with Cornelius. She'd come out of her shell alright, our raised eyebrows communicated.

"It's okay, Tracy. Well, folks, as you all know, I'm a seasoned negotiator. I managed to agree with the hotel that we should stay right here until the storm clears."

"Stay in this shack? Heck, no thanks. Come on, Hat," Rafe grunted. He opened the door, or attempted to, but the wind and rain was a force against it and Rafe struggled to get it open just a few centimetres. Even with an opening that small, the rain got in and immediately soaked Rafe, who groaned as if he was in a battle and under enemy fire.

"Listen to me for once, man! We're to stay here. The storm is dangerous. We're safe here," Maximilian shouted, and he pushed his way through the Hut and pulled the door closed.

He and Rafe glared at each other and I worried that things may become physical. It would be hard to bet which man would win. Maximilian was bigger, but I suspected he was used to using his words and his money as his weapons, not his fists. But could any man with a name like Rafe have fighting skills? I wasn't sure about that.

"Look, this is silly. We'll be back at the hotel in no time. All we have to do for now is sit tight," I said.

"Sit? There aren't even chairs!" Hattie whined.

"Oh, Hat, stop moaning. My fiancé is lying dead out there and you're unhappy because you've got to stand up for a bit?" Yasmine asked.

Hattie at least had the decency to look down at the sandy boardwalk floor in shame.

Everyone sank into an uncomfortable silence. Nobody was happy to be in the Hut, but the rain pummelling the walls and roof was a good reminder of what the alternative was.

"Emily, can I talk to you?" Yasmine asked. She weaved across to the store cupboard without waiting for me to answer. Once we were inside, she closed the rickety door and looked at me, her eyes wide and mournful.

"How are you doing?" I asked. Stupid question, but I was British. I couldn't *not* ask how she was.

She shrugged and a shiver ran down her body. "I'm not going to pretend that Skye was my soulmate. I know as well as everyone else that it was a marriage of convenience. We were both stars, and we wanted to shine even brighter. It would have ran its course in a few years max. The engagement was a... a business decision, let's say."

"You cared for him. I know you did," I argued.

"Sure. Spend enough time and you'll start to care for anyone at all, Emily. I just want you to know that I'm not the grieving widow, and I don't intend to put on that act. I like to think that everything happens for a reason. Maybe Wayne being here is..."

"What?" I asked.

"Maybe it's fate."

"You do seem to be getting on well," I accepted.

Yasmine smiled involuntarily. Just the thought of him brought her more happiness than Skye's death brought her sadness.

"What did you want to talk to me about?" I asked. I was sure she hadn't asked me in the store cupboard just to gush about Wayne. And if she had, I was uncomfortable with her timing.

The smile disappeared from her face and she took a deep, shuddering breath. "Skye's still lying out there, Em. In the rain! In the thunder! I know you said you're not like an amateur sleuth or anything... but..."

"I'm just here on holiday, Yasmine," I mumbled.

"...you're the closest we've got. Please, Em? I know you liked him. He was a flirt, and he was cheeky, but he was also so charming, and he had a soft spot for you."

My cheeks flamed. Flattered by the attentions of a dead man.

"I'm not flattering myself for a moment to believe that Skye Portillo was really interested in someone like me," I admitted, my voice resolute. I was an average woman with a distinctly average life. Skye had either been such a relentless flirt that he couldn't change his behaviour around any woman with a pulse, or he was somehow mocking me. Or maybe it was something else entirely. But it definitely wasn't genuine interest he had shown in me. I was certain of that.

Yasmine rolled her eyes. "He tried to find you on Facebook."

"He... wait... what?"

She smiled, her expression sincere. "He has a secret profile. Only his family and closest friends know about it. He sat up last night trying to find you."

"I don't really have social media," I admitted. True, I'd seen the social media platform, but I hadn't gone so far as to set up an account. Or a profile. Whatever they were called.

"I told him as much. And good for you, by the way. It's really nothing but a glittery pile of steaming horse..."

"Hold on," I interrupted. "Sorry. But hold on. Skye was trying to find me online? While you were with him? I don't get it."

"He liked you, Em. And maybe I should be jealous about that, but I know as well as everyone else that he was never in love with me. I know you liked him too."

I took a long, shaky breath. "Yasmine, you probably won't even believe this, but I've never liked anyone. Well, I've had crushes, but not many. I was raised to... well, that's another story. My mum... she was..."

"It's okay. I get it. And I'm not saying you and Skye would have lived happily ever after. He'd probably have broken your heart at some point. Let's not pretend the guy was an angel just because he's dead. But he deserves justice, right?"

"Of course! And the police will..."

Yasmine tutted. "You believe that Pedaro guy's going to come out here on a white horse like the cavalry? Come on, you're a smart girl. You know that's not going to happen.

Derrick and Skye will just be two rich Americans who came out to Mexico and never went home."

I shifted awkwardly on my feet. I didn't want to admit it, but I suspected she was right. Pedaro and Jiminez hadn't left me with any faith that they'd solve Derrick's murder, and I couldn't see that things would change now there was another killing to deal with.

"You want my help?"

"I want you to solve this case. Your dad's told me all about the murders you've solved, and I think it's crazy cool. People say it's the quiet ones you need to watch, and I guess they're right! You're mad talented, Em."

"I don't know about that," I mumbled. "But, I need to tell you something."

"Anything."

"Cornelius isn't my dad. He's my uncle. We're on this trip together because my mum came out to Mexico when she was younger. She's passed now, and I guess Uncle C thinks there's a side to her that I never knew. We're following in her footsteps."

"Wow. That's so cool! You're so lucky to have an uncle like him. He's hilarious!" Yasmine gushed. "You know, you could totally turn this trip into a reality show! I can speak to my producer? Hook you up?"

"Thanks, that's really kind, but I'm okay keeping this trip just between me and him."

"Oh. Okay. Sure. And your dad? He's back at home?"

"I guess so. We've kind of drifted apart since we lost mum," I admitted, the words sticking in my throat like molasses. The admission felt shameful, as if his absence was somehow because I didn't care enough or had lost his phone number. It was careless to lose a beloved toy, to lose my page in a book, but to somehow completely lose a father? Reckless. Utterly reckless.

"Oh, honey," Yasmine murmured, and she scooped me into a big hug. I didn't even realise I was crying until she discreetly moved her glossy, straight hair out of reach from my snotty nose. With a shuddering breath, I composed myself and met her gaze. She was a celebrity, an icon, but as she stared into my eyes with compassion, she was simply a new friend. And how on earth could I say no to a friend?

"Okay," I said.

"Okay?"

"I'll help."

11

"What am I missing here? Someone wanted to hurt Derrick and Skye. Could they have any enemies in common?"

Yasmine wrinkled her nose in distaste. "Derrick had stacks of enemies. But Skye was adored by everyone. Even the women he'd loved and left. He had that charm, you know?"

I nodded. I could believe that. There *was* something so lovable about Skye, I could imagine the trail of heartbroken women still managing to reserve a soft spot for him in their affections.

"I hate to say this, Yasmine, but you're the common link."

She gasped, her eyes wide. I wondered if she had always been so expressive or whether that was a habit she'd perfected for the TV.

"They're both romantically linked to you," I explained.

"Does that mean that Wayne's next? We need to protect him!"

I'd already reached that conclusion, and had whispered to Uncle C to supervise the rest of the wedding party as the

storm raged on. A quick glance on his news app had shown
that the storm was predicted to get worse, a lot worse, before
it cleared in several hours' time.

As much as I didn't want Yasmine believing that I was
some Miss Marple protege, I had to admit that there wasn't
much else to do to occupy the time than try my hand at
solving the murders.

"He's fine with Cornelius, don't worry. You and Wayne
seem to have got close again very quickly. Are you sure you
hadn't been in touch before he arrived here?"

"No! Not since the split. I wanted to reach out, but what
could I have said? The news were saying such awful things
about me and they were all true!"

"And you're sure you didn't know he was going to join
you out here?"

"I swear! Gosh, if I'd known I'd have packed the little
polka dot bikini he loved."

"Really?" I asked.

She shrugged. "Every girl wants to look her best in front
of her ex, right?"

"Erm... sure, I guess. Okay, I'm going to speak to Wayne
first. Can you ask him to come in here?"

"Hold on. Why are you starting with Wayne? Does that
mean something?"

"Nothing at all. I've got to start somewhere," I lied.

Yasmine nodded and returned to the main space of the
Champagne Hut. From the merry noises coming from in
there, I guessed that a bottle or two had been opened to
help pass the time.

I groaned. I didn't want to be spending my holiday investigating a double homicide, and I especially didn't want to
be interviewing suspects who were drunk.

Wayne looked sheepish as he entered the store

cupboard. His arms were folded and he couldn't quite meet my gaze. Interesting.

"You don't have to talk to me, you know, but your co-operation will be..."

"I know I don't have to. You're not with the police, right?"

I shook my head. "Definitely not with the police."

"You're speaking to me because you think I killed them, right?"

"I... erm..."

He finally lifted his gaze and his eyes locked with mine. It was easy to see why Yasmine found him so appealing. There was something manly about him in a traditional, old fashioned way. Just a look at him told me he didn't put much value on the celebrity industry, and I guessed he was a man with a skin care routine less time intensive than Uncle C's.

"I didn't do it," he said, his voice barely a whisper.

"Well answer my questions and help me figure out who did. First of all, what makes you so sure you should be a suspect?"

He laughed and held up his palms. He had honest hands, hands that had seen hard work as my father would say. "With Skye out of the way, maybe I'll get Yasmine back."

"Hmm. That might seem like an obvious solution, but it doesn't make sense. Who ended your relationship?"

"I did," he admitted. He was telling the truth. Cornelius' various online searches didn't agree about many things, but they did agree that Yasmine Cunningham had been well and truly ditched by Wayne Jones. Some newspapers had ran front page articles calling him the biggest idiot of the century, among other, less friendly things.

"And did you even know Derrick? What would you have to gain from killing him?"

A smile crossed his lips. "I don't know, killing Derrick

would have been satisfying in a way. I'd only met him once before but Yas had told me the things he did to her."

"So you join the line of suspects in relation to Derrick, but it's not a short queue and you're not skipping to the front of it. Look, Wayne, I wanted to speak to you first but not because I think you did it."

"You think I'll be next," he said with a smile as he dragged a finger across his neck, an imitation of him being a dead man walking.

"I think it's possible," I confessed.

"Well, whoever our killer is, they'd be pretty stupid to try it in such a small space. Talk about witnesses! Unless you're the killer and you've got me in here as a pretence for bumping me off?"

I rolled my eyes. "I think you're safe in here. I also think you've done a good job of avoiding my questions so far. Tell me again, who invited you here?"

"I have no idea. I received an invitation in the post. I assumed Hattie and Rafe had sent them."

"Didn't it seem strange to you?"

Wayne cocked his head. "Not really, to be honest. Look, Yasmine doesn't know, but I kept in touch with the family. Damson mainly. We always had quite a bond. She was like a little sister to me. It didn't seem fair to just disappear from her life when I ended things with Yas."

"So you're suggesting that the invite could have come from Damson?"

"No, I'm telling you I assumed Hattie had invited me, and it didn't seem that strange. I kept in touch with her too, not as often as Damson. We messaged here and there."

"Yasmine doesn't know this?"

"Not from me, no. I have no idea if Hattie told her."

"And Damson?"

"Almost certainly she wouldn't tell Yasmine," he said.

"How can you be sure?"

"Well... Damson's different. She loves her family, but she doesn't want the life they've created. I think she saw me as a regular person, a connection with the real world."

"What did you talk about with her?"

He shrugged. "Just stuff. I'd tell her about the walks I go on with my dogs - that's what I do for work, I walk dogs. Or I'd moan about how the price of milk has gone up. It was just really, really dull stuff. She loved it. I was like a window to another world, I guess. All that kid dreams of is studying, having a career, marrying... erm, settling down."

"She does seem awfully uncomfortable with the cameras," I admitted. I'd witnessed that with my own eyes just over the course of the last few days.

"I can't blame her. And she has an advantage. They all do. Yas paved the way for them and created enough interest and enough money that they can all follow their dreams. For Damson, that's a quiet, everyday life."

"I wonder how long it will keep her interest," I reflected. Liking the idea of being a normal person was probably very different from being immersed in the day-to-day monotony.

"We'll see," he said with a grin.

"Okay, so you being here isn't a huge surprise I guess. But what about Derrick? Who do you think invited him?"

Wayne scoffed. "Oh, man. I have no idea about that. I can't imagine any of the Cunninghams wanting to have him back on the scene, sniffing around."

"He was bad news?"

"One hundred percent. I can't stand here with you and pretend to be upset about his demise. Skye's another story. He seemed okay."

"He was a ladies' man. He'd probably have broken Yasmine's heart," I said.

He grinned. "If she didn't break his first, you mean? Those two knew what they were signing up for with each other. It was a match made in headlines."

I sighed. Wayne was nice, really nice, but he didn't have much at all to tell me that was helpful. The fact was, he wasn't in the inner circle, and he didn't even follow the news.

"Hey! Wait! What about while you've been here? Have you seen anything suspicious?" I asked. The question was borne out of desperation. Surely, if he had anything important to tell me, he'd have lead with it. But miracles did happen occasionally. Or so I chose to believe.

"Hmm, not really," he said after taking a moment to ponder the question.

"I guessed not," I admitted.

"You know about the argument, right?" He was already heading towards the door when he asked this, the words tossed casually over his shoulder.

"The... what?"

"Skye and Rafe argued last night. Someone else must have mentioned it to you?"

I frowned. "I don't believe so. Who knows about it?"

"Well, everyone I guess. Skye was mouthing off that he'd tell everyone what Rafe was capable of. Maybe he didn't tell them after all?"

"Maybe he didn't get chance," I muttered as a raucous laugh came from the Champagne Hut. I wondered if supervision duties were not in Uncle C's collection of talents.

"When you put it like that... that's horrid."

"Tell me everything about the argument," I commanded.

Wayne let out a sigh. "I was heading to my room after I checked in. The two of them were out in the corridor, arguing. That's all there is to it."

"What were they arguing about?"

"I have no idea. I saw them, turned and walked the other way. I didn't want to get dragged into whatever it was."

"But you're sure it was Skye and Rafe?"

Wayne nodded. "And it was definitely Skye threatening to tell people what Rafe was really like."

"Wait. Tell people what he was like or what he was capable of?" I picked up on the inconsistency in his story and wondered if it was important.

"Oh... erm... it could have been either, I guess. I'm sorry. I had no idea it would be important. I just wanted to get out of there before they saw me."

"And did you manage it?"

"I think so. Neither of them mentioned it to me today. I even asked Skye earlier if everything was okay."

"What did he say?"

"What would you say if your partner's ex started asking you questions like that? He brushed it off. He was always a little weird around me."

"Jealous?"

Wayne laughed and ran a hand through his hair. "I doubt that. He was just more comfortable with the ladies. He probably liked me fine."

"Okay. Well, thanks Wayne. I'm done with my questions for now. I'll walk out with you," I said.

Wayne held the door open for me and we emerged into the Champagne Hut's main space. LuAnn sat on the sandy floor, a bottle of champagne uncorked in her hands. Her cheeks flushed as she saw me, and I realised that seated next to her was none other than Uncle C. The rosiness of his own face told me that LuAnn hadn't been enjoying the drink alone, and I tried to meet my uncle's gaze but he was - deliberately, I suspected - looking anywhere but at me.

"Everything's fine out here," Yasmine whispered in my ear. I smiled at her gratefully and assessed the situation. With Uncle C well and truly off duty, I had little choice but to trust Yasmine to keep an eye on things for me.

"LuAnn, can I have a word?" I asked.

"Moi?" She asked, then giggled.

"Please," I confirmed. I needed to speak to her before she drank any more.

She climbed up from the sandy floor with my uncle's help, the two of them sharing a laugh that suggested they'd been caught being naughty.

Once in the store cupboard, I directed her to one of the empty drinks crates, which she collapsed into gratefully.

"Emily, Emily, Emily... your father is delightful! Have I told you that before? I bet you hear it all the time. He was just telling me some of the stories of his life. What a life!" LuAnn gushed.

"Yes, well, I'm glad the two of you are enjoying yourselves," I said.

LuAnn took the point and the smile disappeared from her face. "Of course, it's such an awful business. Cornelius is a dear man, trying to distract me. But, yes, this is a serious occasion. I'll be happy to answer your questions."

"Well, that's good. Thank you. First, do you know who invited Wayne and Derrick?"

"Wayne? What's he got to do with it? He's alive, isn't he?"

"Yes, he is... but he and Derrick both seem to have come along without invitations," I explained.

"They did have invitations. They must have. How else would they have got here?"

"Yes, I know they had invitations. I think we're confusing each other. Let me start again. Who invited them?"

"Who invited who?" LuAnn asked. I couldn't decide whether she was genuinely confused, being sarcastic, or was more drunk than I'd realised.

"Who invited Wayne and Derrick?" I clarified.

"Oh. That's no mystery. The production crew did that," she said with a smile, as if relieved to get a question right.

"The production crew? Do the rest of the family know that?" I asked.

LuAnn shrugged. "Probably? Maybe not? I'm the one who deals with those kinds of decisions... scripting, and things."

"But there isn't any scripting? The camera crew just record what you do, don't they?"

"Well, yes, generally speaking. But that could be pretty boring if it's all that happened. People aren't really that interesting, are they? So the production crew give a push every now and then."

"What kind of push?"

"Well, the invitations would be one example. They like to get involved and create dramatic situations, see how we deal with them. It could be that they arrange for an old enemy to turn up at the same event the girls do... things like that."

"And you help them make those decisions? Or they run them by you?"

LuAnn laughed. "Not always. They want that element of surprise, it makes more compelling TV."

"But you did know that Wayne and Derrick were coming to the wedding? That the production team had invited them?"

LuAnn frowned. "No. No, I didn't know about Derrick. I

only found out about Wayne a few hours before he arrived. Personally, I was glad about that. I don't want to speak ill of the dead, but he's the man for Yasmine."

"Okay, but you don't know that the production crew invited Derrick?" I asked.

"Who else could it have been?"

I sighed. "I don't know. That's what I'm trying to find out. Wayne seemed to imagine that Damson or even Hattie had invited him."

"Well, I can't comment on that. I found out that Wayne was attending, I can't say who invited him. I just thought it was the production team. They add something to every series finale. Last season there was Tracy turning up to my birthday party, the season before that we had Derrick turn up and reveal to Wayne that Yasmine was having an affair. That kind of thing."

"Hold on. Derrick told Wayne about it?" I asked. Interesting that Wayne hadn't shared that little bit of information.

LuAnn nodded. "You didn't know that?"

"I don't really keep up with TV shows... or magazines," I admitted.

"Sensible girl. You're like my Damson, your head is screwed on right. I'm glad she's not here, you know. She'd find it very upsetting."

"Being stuck out here in the storm?"

"Gosh, no, not that. She'd find the murders so upsetting. She's a sensitive one."

"Yes, I can imagine. Are you sure that it was Derrick who broke the news to Wayne?"

"I'm certain. I was in the room. The whole thing made it into the series finale, you can see for yourself," LuAnn confirmed. As she nodded her head, her earrings jingled.

"Hmm," I pondered.

"Is that important?"

"I don't know," I admitted. It did give Wayne motive to want to hurt Derrick, but why would he have held onto that anger for years? And it did nothing to create a motive for him to want to hurt Skye... unless he wanted him out of the way so that he could reconcile with Yasmine.

"Well, I'm sure I don't know if you don't. Are you finished with me?"

"Yes, go on. Thank you," I said. LuAnn jumped up and disappeared without a moment's hesitation, as if she wanted to make sure she was gone before I changed my mind and called her back in.

12

I sighed. LuAnn wasn't too inebriated to help, it was just clear that she knew nothing. Or that anything she did know, she wasn't about to share.

Sure, Yasmine was the one who had been discovered, but it was LuAnn's guidance and management that had allowed the transition from one beautiful girl to a family that became a brand.

Truth was, I was nervous of LuAnn. I looked at her and saw a woman so capable of achieving what she wanted, it made me doubt everything, including even my own name.

The door opened and Uncle C barged in, his face red and his pupils dilated. He leaned against the doorway, which strained with his weight, and hiccuped.

"I've been thinking, lassie, I'll help you with the questioning," he slurred.

"Don't you think it's best that one of us supervises... actually, forget that. Come in," I said with a wry smile. Cornelius and I had different ideas of what constituted supervising our collected murder suspects, and he would probably be more use in here with me.

"That's the spirit! We'll rattle through the rest of them before the storm finishes, then we can handcuff the blighter and traipse them across the sand for Pedaro and his man Jiminez to arrest!" Cornelius exclaimed, as he rubbed his hands together and gave out a maniacal laugh.

"Okay, well, come and sit down before you fall over. You've had quite the laugh out there with LuAnn, it seems!"

Cornelius collapsed into a crate, which creaked but held. He eyed me, as much as he could for a man whose eyebrows covered a lot of his line of vision. "Undercover!"

"Huh?" I asked.

"I was undercover!"

"Okay," I dragged the word out, hoping the time would give me some idea of what else to say, but no, I remained blank.

"Emily, listen well. This is an important life lesson. I first learned it back in 1970, it was a hot summer that year and I was working the night shift with my pal, Boney Maroney."

I suppressed a giggle. Cornelius eyeballed me.

"Sorry. You were saying?"

"We were staking out the Banshee Club, which you'd have heard about if you were around at the time, but it's been deleted from history now. Let's just say, too many big names had big secrets at the Banshee Club. Boney and I, we were working a job, he was a private eye you see, and I helped him out now and then. He'd get me in for the cases he was stuck on. This one was a real misfit job!"

A light rap on the door to the cupboard interrupted his story, and Cornelius and I both looked up as the door opened. Rafe looked in at us.

"Have you done, then? Have you spoken to all of the suspicious people?"

"Erm, no. We're speaking to everyone," I clarified.

Rafe looked disappointed. "Everyone? Even Hattie? She's a blooming wreck out here, she is."

"Send her in. We'll speak to her next," Cornelius called out, then glanced at me. "Is that okay?"

"That's fine," I said.

"Oh. Right. Okay," Rafe said, then disappeared from view for a moment. He returned, with Hattie, and the two of them walked into the cupboard and stood awkwardly, hand in hand. Hattie did look nervous.

"One at a time, please. We'll speak to you next, Rafe," I said.

Hattie's eyes widened. "Can't he stay with me? I don't have anything to hide from him."

"We need to speak to each of you alone," I said.

"You're not police, though, are you? You can't force any of us to talk, never mind say we have to be alone to do it," Rafe argued.

"We're not police, lad, but we'll see the police later and we'll tell them who co-operated and who didn't," Cornelius said with a hard glare.

Rafe laughed. "What will they care? They'll probably tell you off for interfering in the first place. Come on Hat, let's leave these jokers to it."

Hattie looked up at me, her eyes wide and damp.

Before she could answer, LuAnn appeared in the doorway, her arms folded. She looked at Rafe, then at Hattie, and addressed them both. "You'll both co-operate and do as you're told. That's an order."

Rafe opened his mouth, but said nothing. After a few moments, he held up his hands and backed out of the room, closing the door behind him.

Hattie took a seat on another discarded crate and looked down at her lap.

"What are you thinking?" I asked.

I expected her to moan about how the murders were ruining her wedding, but instead she took a shaky breath and said, "I'm thinking this is all my fault."

"How so?" Cornelius enquired.

"I should never have invited him."

"Derrick?"

Hattie's head sprang up and she met my gaze. "Good Lord, no! Not him! Wayne... I invited Wayne."

"And what's that got to do with anything?" I asked.

Hattie shrugged lazily. "You think he's the killer, right? You spoke to him first... it makes sense, I guess."

"You think he's capable of killing Derrick and Skye?"

"Anyone's capable of murder, Emily. We all have our limits, and I guess Wayne reached his."

I frowned. Hattie knew Wayne much better than I did. As much as I didn't believe he was the killer, I was aware that I could simply be underestimating him.

Many a serial killer delayed their capture because they were fine looking, or charming; sometimes both.

"He's slipped in your estimation pretty quickly if one minute you were inviting him to your wedding and the next, you believe he's a killer," I pointed out.

Hattie let out a long, unsteady breath, then glanced behind her to check that the door was firmly closed. "I'm not going to judge him, okay? Don't judge until you've walked a mile in his shoes, right? That's the saying? Well, all I know is he was part of the family for a while and we agreed he should be here."

"We? You and who?"

"Rafe and I, of course. We consult each other on all decisions."

"Of course. I'm guessing you had no idea that this would happen, that he'd hurt anyone? If that's what happened?"

"Of course not! And it did happen. Who else had a reason to hurt Skye?"

"What would Wayne's motive be to hurt Skye?"

"Jealousy, of course! He's never got over Yasmine!"

"Interesting that you don't question anyone's motive to hurt Derrick," Cornelius pointed out.

Hattie rolled her eyes. "You two had only just met him, and you'd probably already got enough reason to want him dead. Some people are just no good, and Derrick was one of them."

"But Skye wasn't? He was cheating on Yasmine, you know," I said.

Hattie laughed. "Of course I know! Everyone knew that, and it was hardly cheating on her. That suggests that there's another woman, that there's feelings involved, that there's secrecy. Skye was open about what he was up to."

"Some people might say that gave Yasmine a good motive to want him dead. Surely, he was making a fool of her?"

"No! He was making her... what's the word... sympathetic."

"Sympathetic?" I repeated.

Hattie nodded her head. "She didn't come out of her split with Wayne very well. The media crucified her. They called her all sorts. She even lost some sponsorship deals. It was bad. She was the pantomime villain, and that affected the deals she was offered. She needed a way to be likeable again."

"And Skye was the answer to that?"

"It worked well for him, too. Every woman in the world has imagined herself on his arm. Perhaps even you, Emily."

My cheeks flushed.

"The public loved them as a couple, but we all knew it was temporary. They'd split at some point, Skye would admit his various hook ups, and Yas would probably go on Oprah and cry."

"Wow. You really did have it all figured out."

Hattie shrugged.

The door opened and I looked up to see Rafe return to the room. As he stood in the open door, I caught a glimpse of LuAnn, eyes closed and mouth open, purring with soft snores.

"Are you okay, Hat?" Rafe asked.

"Oh, darling! It's been awful!" Hattie exclaimed. She burst into tears instantly and Rafe dashed across to her, allowing the door to close behind him.

"What have you been doing to her?" Rafe demanded.

I looked at him and frowned. "We've been chatting."

"It's just... it's all so awful!" Hattie wailed, and I resisted the urge to roll my eyes. I glanced at Cornelius, which was risky as his face - and his voice - usually made it clear exactly what he was thinking.

"Let's all take a minute and calm down. It is awful, you're right. That's why you're in here helping us. And *you* might as well sit down, you're making the place look untidy," Cornelius boomed.

Rafe appeared to consider his options, then lowered himself down onto the crate. Hattie nestled into his chest and he shushed her and fussed at her hair.

"Hattie will be fine out there while we talk to you," I said.

"I can't leave her in this state. Has she been like this the whole time? You can't put any stock on her words, if so! She's in no fit state to be..."

"She's been fine, lad. Now, let go of her and we can get this over with a lot quicker," Cornelius said.

Rafe dropped his arms, and Hattie wiped her nose on his t-shirt, then bid a hasty retreat out to the Champagne Hut, where more than just LuAnn's snores were clearly audible.

"Well? What did she tell you?" Rafe asked.

"We're the ones asking the questions," I said.

He shook his head. "She's never on her own. Her whole life is managed, by the production crew, by her mother! I can't stand to think of her in here, alone."

"She managed fine," I softened a little. His concern for her was touching. I wondered if I'd ever have a man so invested in my wellbeing.

"She managed better than fine. She gave us some cracking insights," Cornelius said with a chuckle and a raised eyebrow.

"Well, like I say, her credibility is a little..."

"Nonsense! She's a smart girl, with two eyes and two ears. She knows what she's seen. What she's heard. Now, enough about her. Let's get down to business."

Rafe sat dead straight, his posture of an award-winning quality. "I'll be happy to help, but I don't know much at all."

"You haven't heard the questions yet," I dead panned.

"Let's start with Wayne. You invited him here, right?" Cornelius asked.

"Wrong."

"Hattie told us otherwise," I said.

Rafe shrugged lazily. "Let's say that my involvement in the wedding hasn't been on the same level as hers. You've heard the old breakfast joke, I assume? You order bacon and eggs. The chicken is involved , but that pig is really committed."

"You're telling me you're a chicken?"

He laughed. "In that example, absolutely. I know my place in a Cunningham wedding and there's no way I'd be brave enough to argue with any of the decisions that Hattie made."

"So you went along with Wayne coming, but you weren't keen on the idea?"

"I saw the possibility of trouble. He and Yasmine were like love's young dream. Everyone in the family wanted them to last forever. Everyone in the country wanted the same thing!"

"So, you had some reservations?"

"I guess. But Hattie's argument made sense. He had been a part of the family. Damson was especially close to him, I believe. Hattie was all about being the bigger person. I was happy to allow it."

"Allow it?"

"That's what I said."

"Interesting choice of phrase," Cornelius rumbled beside me.

"What can I say? We're a traditional couple. She looks to me for approval. As I've said already, she needs guidance. She's had that from her family all her life, and soon it will be my job to provide it."

"You make her sound like a child," I said.

"She is in many ways. They all are. In fact, show me a celebrity who isn't! The agents and managers baby these people in a way that is entirely unhelpful."

"You're not a fan of the celebrity industry?"

"Oh, no. I didn't say that. I love a headline as much as the next person. It just... it comes with pros and cons, as any line of work does."

"You've managed to avoid the pitfalls?"

"Some of them. I'm sorry, how are these questions relevant? There are two dead men and you haven't asked me about either one yet."

"You're right. My apologies. We were getting to it," I assured him.

"Did you kill them?" Cornelius barked.

He was going for the element of surprise, but Rafe didn't so much as flinch. He greeted the question with a lazy smile.

"Well?" Cornelius asked.

"What reason would I have to kill either of them? They were both attention seekers, both examples of the common celebrity who likes their own name and their own fame a little too much."

"So, not a fan of either of them?"

"Skye was a laugh. Derrick was a bore. He had a nasty side too."

"Derrick?" I asked.

Rafe nodded. "He had some revealing images of Yasmine. Ones that he hadn't leaked to the press as yet. Called them his pension plan, he did."

"He told you this when? Here?"

"By the pool that morning before he was killed."

"That could have been your motive to kill him, then," Cornelius suggested.

Rafe shrugged. "I guess so. If I cared enough about Yasmine to want to protect what's left of her dignity. I don't, just to clarify. But it does make me wonder whether Wayne did it. He's clearly still smitten with her, don't you think?"

That was a hard point to argue, but I didn't want to agree with a suspect.

"And then he killed Skye so he could reconcile with Yasmine! It makes sense, right?"

"Hmm," I pondered. It did make sense. In fact, it made sense a little too well for my liking.

"He is the obvious suspect," Cornelius agreed.

"Yes, I thought so! Not that I'm pretending I'm a detective like you pair, of course. I assume he's denied it?"

"Well, yes," I admitted.

Rafe nodded and grinned. "That's exactly what the murderer would do!"

"In fairness, it's also what innocent people would do when asked if they'd killed someone."

"Gosh. Yes. That hadn't occurred to me. You've got your work cut out for you, haven't you?"

"Hold on, listen to that!" Cornelius boomed as he jumped up from his crate with a creak of his joints.

"What?" I asked. I could still hear some snoring, but nothing more.

"Exactly! The storm's finished!"

I grinned, despite the seriousness of the situation. "Yes! We can go and fetch help now. We can get Skye taken somewhere a little more respectful than him just lying out in the sand."

We had no chance to react because voices came from outside.

13

"Open the door and walk out, one by one, your arms in the air! This is a police order!"

I groaned.

"Guess who's back!" Cornelius asked as he rubbed his hands together with glee.

"Pedaro," I muttered.

"He must be spitting feathers to be called back here!"

Rafe rose from his chair and we did the same. The rest of the party had already started filing out, and we followed them, our arms stretched up towards the sky, which had miraculously returned to its bright blue state. It was almost as if we had imagined the storm.

I watched as Becker sprinted across the sand with his arms still in the air, and ran into the arms of a familiar figure.

"Damson?" I asked.

"What is this?" LuAnn asked, her attention focused on the rather intimate embrace her youngest child was all too happily involved in.

"You didn't know?" Tracy asked with a sweet-as-sugar smile.

LuAnn turned to her and looked at her sternly. If a look could kill, we'd have a triple murder case on our hands.

"Mom... I should have told you," Damson said as she pulled herself from Becker. Their hands remained linked.

"Told me what exactly?"

"You can work it out from here, surely. Come on, LuAnn. You remember what young love is like?" Maximilian asked with a grin.

Tracy swatted at him, suspecting his own young love memories were wrapped up with the first Mrs Cunningham.

"We're in love, momma. Becker's coming to Cambridge with me. We're going to get our degrees and then marry," Damson's voice wavered as she spoke, but her eyes shone.

Pedaro began to give a slow round of applause.

"Sorry. We can talk about this later," Damson said as her cheeks flushed.

LuAnn glared at the officer. "You've kept us waiting long enough! Another minute won't hurt."

With that, she stormed across the sand to her youngest daughter and her beau, looked from one to the other, then pulled them both in for a hug.

"You're not mad?" Damson asked.

"I love you more than anything in the world. You could never make me mad," LuAnn whispered.

"See? I told you it would be okay," Becker said.

"Not so fast, boy. If you ever so much as think of hurting my daughter, I'll torture you so badly you'll wish for death. Okay?"

He gulped, then nodded. "Okay. Yes, ma'am."

"Looks like our work here is done then. Good day to you all," Pedaro said with a grunt.

"Wait! Damson, why are they even here?" I asked, as I realised that the officers seemed even less concerned than they usually did.

Damson shrugged. "You'd been gone a long time. The hotel insisted on calling these fine officers out to help me find you."

"That's the only reason they're here? To look for us?" I asked.

"What else would we be here for? You have something to confess to, lady?" Pedaro asked with a smirk on his face.

"No! Goodness, no. But there has been a second murder. You'll find the bo- the victim - behind the hut."

Pedaro and Jiminez glanced at each other, their faces a mix of boredom and disappointment.

"You are more senior, jefe," Jiminez said with a shrug.

"I need to watch this group. You go," Pedaro ordered.

"But patron, surely you need to go. A junior officer like me, I'm bound to mess up the scene..."

Pedaro sighed. "Fine, you stay here."

The senior officer moved stealthily around the side of the hut, his gun drawn. He was gone merely seconds when he returned and gave a sombre nod in his colleague's direction.

"Dead?" Jiminez asked, apparently unable to translate the meaning of the nod.

"As a dodo," Pedaro confirmed.

"That's your professional opinion?" Cornelius asked with a waggle of his eyebrows.

"We're going to take you all down to the station. Some time in a Mexican prison cell might help you co-operate a little more," Pedaro said.

"There's no need for that," I interrupted. "I know who did it."

14

"Okay Miss Marple, we'll play along. Tell us what you know," Pedaro said with a cool smile.

I swallowed. All of the wedding party looked at me, their attention for once fixed on something other than their own fame.

"So first of all, we had Derrick Riches killed. That was tricky because it seemed as if nobody liked him. The person with the biggest motive would have appeared to be Yasmine. He had treated her badly."

"What? I thought you were my friend!" Yasmine exclaimed. Her eyes filled with tears and I was touched to see that she appeared to be genuinely hurt.

"I said you would appear to be the prime suspect, not that you were. Yes, Derrick had done you wrong, but he'd also created the opportunity for you to start your career. Not to mention the fact that his wrongdoings were years ago. If you'd wanted to hurt him because of them, you'd have done it back then."

"I would have! Maybe I should have!" Yasmine muttered.

"Then I wondered about your mum," I admitted.

"Me?" LuAnn asked with a giggle. She was still drunk, and had managed to sidle across the sand and sprawl herself across Cornelius, who had a dopey grin on his face.

"You're so protective of your whole family. I wondered if you'd hurt Derrick as a way of getting revenge for what he did to Yasmine."

"I wouldn't put it past me," LuAnn admitted, with a hiccup.

"The problem with Derrick's death is that almost everyone had a motive to kill him. Everyone apart from Rafe, who seemed to dislike him but had no particular issue with him."

Rafe shrugged. "I was annoyed about what he did to Yasmine, of course I was."

"But you weren't, really? Were you? Certainly not enough to kill for it."

Rafe's skin blanched. "Goodness. No. No, I wasn't upset enough to kill him because of that."

"I thought not," I said with a smile.

"It was really Skye's death that made things fall into place, wasn't it, lassie?" Cornelius called.

"It was, you're right. Skye was a ladies' man, but everyone seemed to like him. Even Yasmine, who knew he was being unfaithful, didn't seem angered by it."

"The relationship was a more commercial decision," Yasmine said. Wayne stood by her side and she could barely take her eyes from him.

"I struggled to get my head around that at first, I'll admit it. But once I had, it made sense. Yasmine's like a puppet master, she's pulling all of these strings. It's very clever. You're thinking five steps ahead of me. I'm focused on Skye being unfaithful today, but your mind is already thinking about the sympathetic headlines you'll get when you have to divorce him."

"Something like that," she agreed. Wayne rolled his eyes.

"Understanding the lengths you go to, to control the narrative, was a big part of cracking the case. Not to mention the production team, and the way they add little sparks to create drama. Like inviting Derrick."

"I guessed it was them," Yasmine admitted.

"They love to put us in a corner and see how we'll react. They might think twice before trying it again!" LuAnn said with a laugh.

"They might. Although a series finale that includes two murders is going to bring in quite the audience," Cornelius said.

"And that's really the key, isn't it? Headlines. Audience. Fame."

"What do you mean?" Hattie asked.

"For most people, a wedding is a private commitment to another person. Sure, there are guests and a dress and flowers, but the most important thing is the creation of a holy bond with another person."

"That's really beautiful," Hattie said. She reached out and grasped Rafe's hand.

"That's become lost here. Or maybe it was never part of it. Hattie, you've orchestrated a wedding that will be watched by millions. Even your romantic walk on the beach included paparazzi. You leaked the details to them, didn't you?"

"Well, I..." Hattie stammered.

"That's an outrageous allegation!" Rafe scolded her and dropped her hand.

"I just... I wanted to offer a little sneak peek before the season finale. I thought we'd..."

"They paid for that sneak peek?" I asked.

Hattie scoffed. "Of course they would have."

"How much?"

"I can't see that those kind of figures have any relevance here," Hattie said through gritted teeth.

"The amount doesn't matter for this conversation. The point is, the focus of this wedding has been forgotten."

"By Hattie, yes," Rafe said.

Hattie said nothing but looked down at the sand.

"Your involvement has been curious, Wayne," I moved on.

He gave a nervous laugh. "I won't argue with you on that point."

"It's clear your feelings for Yasmine are still there."

"She's the love of my life. I've never said otherwise," he admitted.

Yasmine blushed by his side.

"Derrick Riches had explicit photographs of her that he planned to release at some point in the future. Were you aware of that?"

His eyes narrowed. "No. I wasn't aware of that. Hadn't that man already done enough?"

"You're angry," I said.

"Not angry enough to kill him. Even if I had known, I wouldn't have resorted to violence."

"So you say. But defending your woman's honour might justify violence. Some would say it does."

"Wayne isn't a fighter," Yasmine said.

"Perhaps not. But once Skye was killed, he became the prime suspect. He was clearing out the competition. Leaving the path free for him to be reunited with his true love."

Wayne gave a lopsided smile. "You're using my words against me. That's smart. But it doesn't make what you're saying true."

"Wayne, honey, if you killed them to defend Yasmine, that's nothing to be ashamed of!" LuAnn slurred.

There was a collective groan as Wayne, Yasmine, Hattie and Damson all rolled their eyes.

"Remember that anything you say may be used as evidence," Cornelius murmured into LuAnn's ear. She grinned at him and snickered.

"I haven't killed anyone," Wayne insisted.

"But it makes such perfect sense. You killed Derrick because he had those photos. Then you killed Skye to clear the way for you to get back with her. It all fits into place."

"Maybe it does, except I didn't hurt anyone, and I didn't even know about any photos!"

"Hmm," I said.

"Are you wrapping this up any time soon? We have other places to be?" Pedaro prompted.

"I'm just coming to it. It's interesting that you didn't know about the photos. Isn't that interesting, Rafe?"

"Is it?" He asked.

"It's just, I find it curious that you're the only one who knew about them."

"He wasn't blackmailing anyone with them right now, he was just making me aware that he planned to. Why would he tell anyone else?"

"It just doesn't add up to me. Derrick Riches was flamboyant, he told everyone everything, and he acted impulsively. If he did have photos, he'd have released them, or he'd have at least threatened Yasmine with them directly."

"Yep. That's the kind of thing Derrick would do,"

Yasmine agreed with a shudder. Wayne pulled her in close for a hug.

"Instead, you suggest that he told you and only you about them."

Rafe shrugged. "I can't control how forthcoming other people are with information."

"Are you suggesting we're lying?" LuAnn exclaimed.

"It could just have been a curious oversight from other people, if not for the fact that that piece of information creates Wayne's motive. Without that, what reason does Wayne have to kill Derrick?"

"Can I just remind you that I didn't kill anyone?" Wayne asked.

I rolled my eyes. "We're talking theoretically. Rafe, and only Rafe, gave Wayne a motive."

Rafe glared at me.

"The theory of Wayne being the killer fit. It fit perfectly, as long as Derrick really did have photographs and someone had made Wayne aware of them. If that was the case, we had our killer, it lined up perfectly. And if I've learned anything, it's that cases don't line up perfectly."

"If it's by the book, give it a second look," Cornelius said with a nod.

"So, do you know who the killer is, or not?" Hattie asked.

"I'm getting there," I said. "Rafe told us that the decision to invite Wayne to the wedding had really been yours, Hattie. Something he'd just gone along with."

Hattie glanced at her fiance, then back at me. She was open mouthed. "Well, I mean, I could have..."

"Then he made an interesting slip of the tongue about him allowing it. It was clear to me that Rafe called the shots in the relationship. Wayne was only here because Rafe wanted him to be."

"Nonsense!" Rafe exclaimed.

"We did talk about it, babe," Hattie murmured.

"Maybe we did. In the middle of the dress and the bridesmaids and the flowers and the venue and everything else you got obsessed about! You were wedding crazy for months, Hat! I couldn't listen to every single thing you said!"

Hattie flinched as if he had struck her, then straightened up and looked at him with a steely gaze. "We did talk about it. I thought Damson would appreciate Wayne being here, but I was worried it might be awkward for Yasmine. You insisted that it was my job to take the high ground and invite him."

"Okay, if you say so," Rafe said in a sing song voice.

"Don't patronise me," Hattie said.

"Don't patronise my daughter," LuAnn said, somehow instantly sobered up.

"You've done lots of things on this trip that have felt a bit off with me. You didn't want Hattie speaking to us alone, did you?" I asked.

"I wanted to protect her. You two are total amateurs and you're playing a dangerous game," Rafe said.

"And then you managed to join her while we were still speaking to her, and you were quick to tell us that anything she might have said wouldn't be credible. Remember that, lassie?" Cornelius asked.

"Oh, yes! I do remember that!"

"You told them that? Why?" Hattie asked. She stepped away from Rafe, crossed her arms, glowered at him.

"Darling, I was just sticking up for you. You're not that great under pressure, are you?" Rafe asked.

"Excuse me? Can I remind you that I am a business owner! An entrepreneur! I run a company and I'm absolutely fine under pressure!" Hattie shouted.

"I hate to interrupt a lover's tiff, but let me wrap this up. Rafe, you were also the one who told us that Derrick had photos of Yasmine. And you were pretty keen that we treat Wayne as the killer. All of those things together were pretty suspicious, but I didn't know how far to take them. Wayne was still the more obvious killer."

"He was, indeed," Cornelius agreed.

"It's possible that Rafe is a jerk, but not a murderous jerk," I said with a shrug and an innocent smile.

"Hey!" Rafe objected.

"Let me ask you again, Hattie. Who organised the paparazzis?"

Hattie glanced at Rafe, then sighed. "I don't know. I know we had offers. I thought we'd turned them down."

"So you were lying just now?"

She looked at her feet. "When we were walking on the beach, Rafe told me it was important I say it was me if I was asked. He said he didn't want my mum judging him for it. I didn't mean to mislead you. I'm sorry."

"Rafe?"

He raised an eyebrow but said nothing.

"You organised the paparazzi because you were desperate to have the headlines be focused on you for a change. You slipped them the key for the Hibiscus Suite. You're a man obsessed with celebrity and you hate being surrounded by people who have more of it than you do."

"Nonsense," he muttered.

"You killed Derrick because you suspected the production crew had invited him here with some agenda to take over the series finale."

"I feel sick," Hattie said, and collapsed onto the sand. Yasmine ran to her and pulled her into an embrace.

"I suspect you weren't listening when Hattie talked

about inviting Wayne. You had no reason to want him here, although he ended up being a good choice to try and frame. You killed Skye because his proposal to Yasmine threatened to take the attention away from you and Hattie."

Rafe scoffed. "And your little investigation's going to stand up in court, is it? These fine officers are going to build a case against me?"

"I can't believe you did it," Hattie murmured. Tears streamed down her face.

"You suspected?" I asked her.

She nodded. "After Derrick's death, Rafe started telling me about the day, about how we'd been together before-hand, holding hands. But I wasn't with him. I thought I must have been misremembering. But you were tricking me into giving you an alibi, weren't you? How could you?"

"Oh, come on. You were as scared as I was that Yasmine would take over the headlines as she normally does!"

"Yes, I was. I'll admit that just for one day I wanted to be the princess. I wanted the fairy tale to be about me. But, God, Rafe, I wouldn't have hurt anyone!"

"And that's why I did! I did it for you! For us!"

"Don't you dare! Don't you dare say this was for me. I don't want their blood on my hands. You're an awful man! I can't believe I ever... I ever loved you!"

"We done here?" Pedaro asked, his tone and expression emotionless.

I nodded. "You can take him away. I'm sure he'll give a full confession to whichever magazine offers the most money."

W e waved goodbye to the Cunningham family as they set off for the airport and their private plane, then retreated to our suite.

Uncle C put the kettle on and I flopped down on the settee.

"That was good work, lassie," he said as he reached for a packet of Lady Grey tea bags that I'd never seen him with before.

"What's that you're drinking?"

His cheeks, or what was left of them that wasn't covered in facial hair, flushed. "Just a little something LuAnn gave me. It's good to try new things."

"Oh, really? So, you'll be keeping in touch with her?" I teased.

"It would be impolite not to. Now, lassie, we have two more nights here and then we must move on. Are you up for a day of doing absolutely nothing tomorrow, by the pool?"

"I can't think of anything better," I said with a grin.

I reached for the remote control and turned on the TV. It went straight to an American entertainment channel, and the headlines were dedicated to the murders of Derrick Riches and Skye Portillo, followed by an exclusive scoop - Yasmine Cunningham was supposedly engaged to her former husband, Wayne Jones.

"Good for them," I murmured.

I was pleased to see that Rafe didn't get as much as a mention.

THE END

Stay up to date with Mona Marple releases and more:
http://www.monamarple.com/vip-readers

Keep reading Emily and Uncle C's series:
mybook.to/mex3

ABOUT THE AUTHOR

Mona Marple is author of the Waterfell Tweed, Mystic Springs and Christmas Mysteries cozy mystery series', a co-author of the Witch in Time series, and author of this Mexican Mysteries series.

She lives in Nottinghamshire, England with her daughter, husband and pampered Labradoodle.

When she isn't writing words, Mona is probably reading them. She also enjoys walking, being by the sea, and spending quality time with her loved ones.

f facebook.com/MonaMarpleAuthor

instagram.com/monamarple

9 781914 296031